"I want more nights like last night," Sam said

He knew he was probably a sucker for trying to nurture something that had "short-term fling" written all over it, but Kasey had turned him inside out in the space of twenty-four hours.

Heat flashed in her eyes. "But you're...you're a client."

"I'll stay completely out of your office. You'll take care of the account and no one has to know that we're having mind-blowing sex at the same time. That will be our little secret," he promised.

Her breathing quickened. "You really won't tell anyone?"

"No one. We'll just get together to discuss the PR campaign and have great sex, and no one will be the wiser." Although that wasn't the way he would have preferred it, Sam could tell the concept excited her. Now, if only his suggestion was convincing enough to get her back into his bed. "What do you think?"

"I think you'd better take me back to the office."

His heart sank. "That's a no?"

She smiled. "It's a yes. And if you don't take me back to work immediately, I might jump you right here...."

Dear Reader,

Whoops, I blinked and twenty years went by! How is that possible? It seems like only yesterday that I sold my first Temptation novel. Back when I was just a child. I guess that cliché about time flying when you're having fun must be true, because I'm having so much fun that time hasn't merely flown by—it's traveled at the speed of light!

And the fact remains, no matter how I flip the calendar around, that my first book, *Mingled Hearts,* Temptation #9, came out in May 1984. Writing for Temptation was a good thing then, and it's an even better thing now.

So consider this book you're holding as the official beginning of my next twenty years. Happy birthday, Temptation!

Warmly,

Vicki Lewis Thompson

Books by Vicki Lewis Thompson

HARLEQUIN TEMPTATION
826—EVERY WOMAN'S FANTASY
853—THE NIGHTS BEFORE CHRISTMAS
881—DOUBLE EXPOSURE
921—DRIVE ME WILD

HARLEQUIN BLAZE
  1—NOTORIOUS
 21—ACTING ON IMPULSE
 52—TRULY, MADLY, DEEPLY
102—AFTER HOURS

VICKI LEWIS
THOMPSON

OLD ENOUGH TO KNOW BETTER

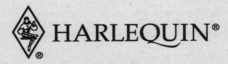

HARLEQUIN®

TORONTO • NEW YORK • LONDON
AMSTERDAM • PARIS • SYDNEY • HAMBURG
STOCKHOLM • ATHENS • TOKYO • MILAN • MADRID
PRAGUE • WARSAW • BUDAPEST • AUCKLAND

The book is dedicated with gratitude to all the Temptation editors who for twenty years have helped make my books the best they can be, with special affection and thanks to Claire Gerus, Margaret Carney, Lisa Boyes, Susan Till, Birgit Davis-Todd and, of course, Brenda Chin.

ISBN 0-373-69180-7

OLD ENOUGH TO KNOW BETTER

Printed in U.S.A.

1

"HOTTIE ALERT!"

Kasey Braddock glanced up. While the two guys in the office made remarks about female chauvinists, all the women hurried to where Gretchen Davies, a gutsy woman with a great laugh, had her nose pressed to the glass of the second-floor window. Moans of appreciation sounded in chorus.

Deciding from everyone's reaction that the view was worth checking out, Kasey punched the save button on her computer and walked toward the window. She'd been working on a PR campaign for a lingerie shop that wanted to shift its image—more Victoria's Secret, less Frederick's of Hollywood.

Hours of careful research on the subject of lace teddies and thong underwear had reminded her that she'd been seriously neglecting the goal she'd set for herself: to become the woman she'd always wanted to be. Sure, she'd worked on her appearance but she had yet to launch her personal campaign to act as sexy as she now looked. The nerd that still lurked inside seemed to be giving orders to the babe she'd become on the outside. Maybe ogling a fine example of Phoenix manhood would jump-start the new Kasey.

"Okay, my turn." She approached the cluster of five

women blocking her view. "Two of you aren't eligible, anyway, so give a single girl a break."

"I was only saving you a good spot." Brandy Larson's fiancé, Eric Lassiter, was out of the office on an appointment, and she looked suitably guilty as she moved aside to make room for Kasey. "Try not to drool on the window," she murmured.

"Hey, Brandy, I'm telling Eric." Ed Finley leaned on the watercooler and observed the commotion.

"Don't go being a tattletale, Ed." Kasey gave him a warning glance, hoping he wasn't serious.

"Aw, I'm just kidding, Kase." Ed flashed her a peace sign.

"Glad to hear it." Kasey held her own in this boisterous office, but she wondered if that would still be the case if everyone knew she was only twenty. She'd finished college at eighteen. After thoroughly evaluating all the PR firms in the Valley, she'd targeted Beckworth, landing the job before her nineteenth birthday. Only the big boss, Mr. Arnold Beckworth himself, knew her age. She wanted to keep it that way, so she'd continue to be treated as an equal.

"Ten bucks says he takes his shirt off in the next five minutes." Gretchen clutched a file folder to her ample chest as she stared outside.

Kasey finally took a look. "My God, it's Tarzan with a chain saw." Right at eye level, a really cute dark-haired guy stood balanced in a large mesquite tree. As the pruned branches toppled to the ground fifteen feet below, a couple of other workers cut them into smaller sections and loaded them into the back of a trailer.

His square jaw clenched, safety goggles making him

look seriously macho, Trimmer Guy gripped his chain saw and made precision cuts. His muscles bunched under a sweat-stained T-shirt.

"I'll take that bet," said Amy Whittenburg, a forty-something divorcee with very red hair. "That's a company logo on the back of his shirt. Ashton Landscaping probably requires their employees to keep the shirts on to promote the company."

"I have to say he's promoting that company in a mighty fine manner," said Myra Detmar, the receptionist. "Mighty fine. Look at those shoulders. Too bad he's wearing gloves. We can't check out his ring finger."

"There you go again, making a sex object out of some poor slob," called Jerry Peters from his desk across the room. "If a bunch of guys acted the way you women act, we'd be crucified." Balding and on the pudgy side, Jerry always chimed in with a dose of indignation during a Hottie Alert.

"Oh, bite me," Gretchen shot back. "Between the insulation and the noise of his saw, he can't hear a word we say, and with the reflective coating on this window he can't even see us. It's like watching a movie."

"More like *Candid Camera*," Jerry said. "I think I'll wander out there and ask him if he knows there's a huddle of rabid females on the other side of the glass pretending he's the star attraction at Chippendale's."

Gretchen turned to glare at Jerry. "You do and you'll never get another double chocolate espresso on my coffee run, bub."

"Well, Tarzan's adorable," said Robbi Harrison, who'd returned from her honeymoon a week ago, "but I'm so spoken for. I'll have to leave him for the rest of you." She walked back to her desk. "I just had to take a peek for old time's sake."

"I tell you, that Ashton Landscaping shirt is comin' off," Gretchen said. "It's gotta be at least ninety out there, and handling that chain saw can't be easy. Look, he's turned it off and propped it in the crotch of the tree."

"I love it when you talk dirty." Kasey winked at her.

Gretchen laughed. "Mark my words, he's thinking about losing the shirt."

"I'm betting another ten that he does," Kasey said, joining in the ever-popular game. She studied the shirt in question. Ashton Landscaping was stenciled on the back in green script. She tried to think why the name Ashton sounded familiar. Even the guy looked like someone she should know. Information was working its way in from the far reaches of her memory, but it wasn't quite there yet.

"As long as we're throwing down bets," said Amy, "we might as well draw straws for him, too, in case he turns out to be available."

"Un-freaking-believable," Jerry muttered. "It's the straws again."

"It's the only fair way to handle a Hottie Alert," Gretchen said. "Robbi, we need you back over here. You can be the designated straw holder."

Kasey's heart began to pound. She'd have to take part in the straw thing or lose face. So far, she'd never ended up with the long straw, so she hadn't been required to go out and ask whatever hottie they were ogling for a date. Mostly she'd been relieved not to be forced into doing it. Then again, maybe peer pressure was the best way to launch her new persona.

"Here you go." Robbi came up beside them. She held out her hand, and four stubs of paper sprouted from her closed fist. "May the best woman win."

Kasey gazed at the stubs of paper. It was like a game of chicken. The idea was for the lucky gal to go out with the guy and make him drool without her handing over the goods. But twice since Kasey had started working at Beckworth, a woman had taken the dare and ended up engaged. Kasey wasn't about to let that happen to her.

Yet she was at a distinct disadvantage considering her age and the fact that until she'd graduated from college she'd been nerd-girl. She wasn't a virgin, but she'd never been assertive with guys and never been in demand. Her first job had seemed like the perfect time to start over and create a whole new Kasey Braddock, though, so far, she'd really done nothing more than change her look.

A long straw would put her goal to change her image to the ultimate test, and maybe it was time. Taking a deep breath, she reached for a stub of paper and hoped for the long straw.

SAM ASHTON LOVED taking a mangy-looking mesquite with good bones and transforming it into a sculptural work of art. He'd turn over other pruning jobs to his workers, but he didn't trust anyone else to make the right cuts on a beauty like this one. Besides, he'd never outgrown the joy of climbing trees.

While he worked, he thought about the woman he'd noticed this morning parking her little red Miata in the lot next to the building. He'd been lounging in his truck drinking coffee while he waited for his employees to arrive at the job site. During down times, he usually thought about ways to boost business.

More business would be good for him, but even better for his little brother's band, which desperately needed a backer. Although Colin and the other band members operated on a shoestring, the Tin Tarantulas had created a Gen-Y fan base in the Phoenix area, and Sam would love to help them buy better equipment and record a demo. They had the potential to make it.

He'd been daydreaming about that when here came trouble, pulling into a space in the next row, lining up exactly in front of him. The red convertible said *look at me*, but as if that weren't enough, the vanity plate announced that the blond woman driving it was SO REDY.

Sam's pulse rate had picked up. He'd always been a sucker for a woman in a red ragtop, and one who announced she was "so ready" had real promise. He'd sipped his coffee as she'd flipped down her visor, pulled off her shades and run a comb through sleek hair that hung straight to the shoulders of her white suit jacket. When she'd dabbed on some lip gloss from an applicator wand, he'd figured it was likely as red as the car, even though he couldn't see for sure.

He hadn't dated much in the past few months, mostly because he was getting picky. These days if a relationship had no potential, he backed away much faster than he used to. At thirty, he didn't care to waste time on dead ends anymore. His last girlfriend hadn't been ready to settle down, partly because of her age.

He had to admit there was a big gap between twenty-three and thirty.

But even though he'd started thinking in terms of the *M* word, he was still a typical guy, and visuals snagged him first. Yeah, he should be willing to ignore the figure and see into a woman's soul. He wasn't quite that evolved yet.

Therefore he'd waited to see what kind of body went with the red car, the shiny hair and the saucy license plate before he committed himself to being interested. At last she'd opened her door. With his first glimpse of leg, his interest had shot up exponentially.

He'd returned his travel mug to its holder in the console and wrapped both arms around the steering wheel as he'd leaned forward. What followed was an outstanding view of the cutest ass ever to grace a bucket seat, wrapped in a short white skirt that was barely legal. Thank God, the mini was still in fashion.

After closing her door, she'd reached over to grab her shoulder bag from the passenger seat. Excellent. Sam watched with relish as the white material stretched across her bottom. Yowza. He'd gazed, enjoyed...and leaned on the horn. Immediately he'd backed off the wheel and the damned horn. He'd driven through a rural area yesterday and a bunch of bugs had done a kamikaze number on his windshield. He'd hoped that would keep her from seeing him clearly.

She'd turned and glanced over at his truck. Fortunately, because of the angle, she wouldn't have been able to see the Ashton Landscaping lettered on the cab doors. He'd picked up the contract for today's job and pretended to study it while he'd kept track of her from the corner of his eye. God, how uncool was that, to accidentally honk the horn. She'd shrugged and started toward the building, her hips swaying, her high-heeled sandals tapping on the asphalt.

Sam let out a breath. Before he finished today, he needed to find out who she was. If nothing else, he could leave a note taped to her steering wheel, but he'd rather talk to her face-to-face. As he pruned the mesquite tree, he wondered where her office might be, which one of the building's tenants she worked for. Too bad the windows all had reflective glass, because from his perch he would be able to see into several of the building's offices.

Then again, maybe the reflective glass was a good thing. If he got another eyeful of her, especially if she happened to be bending over a file drawer, he might tumble right out of the tree. She was one hot babe.

And speaking of hot, thinking about her while working like a farm animal had spiked his internal temperature. Sweat stung his eyes and rolled down his spine. Life would be a hell of a lot more pleasant without his shirt.

After turning off the saw, he propped it carefully in the crotch of the tree. Then he took off his work gloves and goggles and tucked them in beside the saw. Finally he braced his knees against the trunk for balance and reached for the hem of his shirt.

KASEY TUGGED on a stub of paper. And tugged, and tugged some more, until she stood holding the eight-inch strip that was clearly the long straw. The other three women groaned with disappointment.

Before Kasey could get her mind around the fact that she'd won, Gretchen gasped. "The shirt!"

All attention focused on the window once again as Tarzan of the Chain Saw took off his goggles, peeled his shirt from his back and draped it over a tree limb. A collective sigh went up from the group of women.

"I can see his ring finger," said Myra in hushed tones. "No ring."

Amy cleared her throat. "Didn't notice. Too busy looking at his body to notice his fingers. Girls, behold a work of art."

"Wouldn't you know." Gretchen gestured toward the window. "There's the answer to my prayers, and here I stand with a freaking short straw."

Kasey's first impulse was to trade straws with Gretchen. This guy was way out of her league. Her dates had been few and far between, but they'd all been with braniacs, not jocks. And not a one of them had possessed a build to equal this. But trading straws was not an option, not if she wanted to polish her so-far-undeserved rep as a happening chick whose license plate announced she was SO REDY. A happening chick would use that long straw to claim her prize.

"He's beyond gorgeous," said Amy. "Look at that. Even a tattoo."

Kasey screwed up her courage to take another look at her challenge du jour, who was currently mopping his face with his shirt. Sure enough, he had a tattoo on his upper arm that looked like a ring of barbed wire.

As she stared at that tattoo, her memory delivered

the information she'd been trying to retrieve ever since her first glimpse out the window. She'd seen that tattoo twelve years ago, wrapped around the arm of her step-brother Jim's high school buddy, a dreamy guy by the name of Sam Ashton.

She could still picture the two teenagers out by the family's budget-sized swimming pool, radio blaring as they worked on their tans before prom. She'd been the eight-year-old brat who'd spent the afternoon splashing them from her vantage point in the pool. Finally Sam had responded, diving in and giving her a thorough dunking.

The cut at the corner of her mouth had been totally her fault. If she hadn't flailed around so much, she wouldn't have whacked herself in the mouth with her secret decoder ring. The minute Sam had noticed she was bleeding, he'd rushed her into the house, both of them dripping all over her mother's clean floor. Then he'd insisted on going with her to the emergency room, where the doctor had given her two small stitches.

Sam had sat right there, even though he'd looked decidedly green during the stitching process. He'd apologized about a hundred times. The next day he'd sent her a bouquet of flowers. That was when she'd fallen hopelessly in love as only an eight-year-old can fall for a sophisticated older man of eighteen.

After that she'd asked Jim endlessly when Sam was coming over again, but apparently finals and graduation had kept him too busy and he hadn't made it back to their house that spring. Then Jim told her Sam's family had moved to Oregon, and that's where Sam would be going to college in the fall. Jim had left to join the

Marines and the two friends had lost touch. Kasey hadn't seen Sam again...until now.

"So, Kasey, what's your game plan?" Gretchen asked.

Kasey blinked, pulling herself from the past, when she'd had a mad crush on Sam, to the present, when she was the designated Bad Girl from Beckworth out to put some serious moves on the guy. Aside from fighting her internal panic, she had to decide if there was the remotest chance he'd recognize her.

Probably not. Jim was her stepbrother, so they had different last names, and what were the chances Sam would remember a little pain in the ass named Kasey? Besides, she didn't look anything like that eight-year-old. The scar was barely visible. Braces for her teeth, straightener for her frizzy blond hair and tinted contacts for her nearsightedness had all made a difference. Hormones and the good advice of Jim's girlfriend Alicia, now his ex-girlfriend, had taken care of the rest.

Kasey had worked hard to look older and more experienced than she was. From her little red car to her sassy clothes, she'd created an image that required her to take charge of this assignment to snare Sam's interest, and take charge fast.

"I think he looks hot, don't you?" she asked Gretchen.

"Oh, honey, don't you know it. And I need to hear what you intend to do about it. We have to live vicariously through you, so tell us your plan."

"No, I mean he looks *really* hot."

"That's what I'm saying! So how are you—"

"I'm going to take him a nice cold bottle of water

straight from the machine in the break room. I'll get his attention first and then toss it up to him.''

Gretchen smiled. ''Brilliant.''

''But then won't he know we've been watching him?'' Myra asked.

''He'll know Kasey's been watching him,'' said Amy, ''and I think that's part of her strategy, right, Kase?''

It hadn't been, but caught off guard, Kasey was happy to gather any words of wisdom on the art of seduction. ''Of course.'' She walked to her desk, grabbed some change from her wallet and headed for the break room, trailed by Gretchen, Myra and Amy.

''How's your throwing arm?'' Amy asked. ''You don't want to heave it up there like a weakling.''

''My arm's good.'' Kasey put the money in the machine and punched the button for bottled water. ''My brother taught me to throw when I was a kid.''

''That's lucky.'' Gretchen nodded as the bottle thumped down the chute. ''A wimpy throw wouldn't help your cause.''

''You'd better get out there quick,'' Myra said. ''He's starting up the saw again. He might not notice you down there if he's cutting tree limbs.''

Sure enough, the whine of the chain saw drifted into the break room. Kasey thought fast. ''Okay, I can deal with that.'' She handed her bottle to Gretchen. ''Hold on to this for a sec, okay?''

''Anything for you, toots.''

Kasey slipped out of her white suit jacket. Underneath she wore a stretch-lace shell that made the most of her breasts.

"That oughta do it," Amy said. "Let him have it with both barrels, kid."

Kasey had never been fond of the word *kid* as a nick-name, maybe because it had been applied to her so often in the past. But she knew Amy didn't mean it literally. Amy thought Kasey was in her mid-twenties, because that's what Kasey had led everyone to believe.

"Thanks," she said. "I will." She took the bottle from Gretchen, then walked back into the office and tossed her jacket over her chair.

She didn't even glance toward the window as she left the office, afraid seeing Sam there looking so yummy would weaken her nerve. The women in the office called after her with words of encouragement, while Jerry and Ed carried on some more about female chauvinists. Those taunts didn't bother Kasey. She'd spent enough time observing her big brother to know that women had a long way to go before they caught up with the guys in that department.

What bothered her was fear, plain and simple. In theory, she was perfectly willing to do her share of ogling and assertive date-making. But to begin with Sam... that was more of a challenge than she could have envisioned in her wildest dreams.

If she could carry this off, though, without his ever knowing that she was the scrawny little pest he'd dunked in the pool all those years ago, that would be amazing. Making Sam drool would be more than a feather in her Bad Girl's cap. Snagging the attention of a guy like Sam would be on the order of a damned plume.

2

ALTHOUGH SAM REQUIRED his workers to wear ear-
plugs when they used the saw, he hated the damn
things, so he fudged and left them out whenever he
could get away with it. Fifteen feet in the air he could
get away with it. That was probably the only reason he
heard Carlos yelling at him over the loud buzz.

Turning off the switch with his thumb, he glanced
down at his assistant. "What?"

"The lady wants to know if you'd like a bottle of water." Carlos gestured to his left.

Sam pulled off his safety goggles and let them dangle
around his neck as he peered through the branches. He
almost dropped his saw. It was her, the woman with
the red Miata.

Her blond hair gleamed in the morning sun. Not
only that, she'd ditched the white jacket. That move
was understandable in the heat, but the resulting view
of twin beauties outlined by stretch lace had Sam grabbing for a tree limb to steady himself.

She lifted her beautiful face toward him, squinting in
the sunlight. "Nice job!"

"Thanks!" Talk about *nice*. He was staring down at
the most wonderful view of nice he'd seen in a
long time.

"I thought you could use some water!" She held up a plastic bottle.

He could use a whole lot more than water. A cold shower would be good, and not because he was sweating, either. His strong attraction to her was a little embarrassing, to be honest. By his age he was supposed to be over this sort of reaction to a pretty girl. He'd seen plenty of pretty girls, even plenty of naked pretty girls. Yet he was mesmerized by this particular woman.

Maybe he'd developed heat stroke. He forced himself to engage in normal conversation instead of the caveman-speak that occurred to him. "Sure," he said. "I'd love some water." Now wasn't the time to let her know he had several bottles of the stuff in a large cooler in his truck.

"I'll toss it up," she said.

"No, I'll come down." The way she'd messed with his concentration, he didn't trust his hand-eye coordination right now. Nothing would be worse than missing the bottle she threw up to him.

Correction. Worse would be missing the bottle and falling out of the tree at the same time. Besides risking serious injury to his body, he could destroy his pride forever, not to mention his chances of dating this woman.

He left the saw propped in the tree. Then he took off the goggles and hung them on a branch before grabbing his shirt and pulling it on over his head. At last he started the climb down.

He'd never descended from a tree in front of an audience before, and self-consciousness made him clumsy. His foot slipped and he nearly fell. Grabbing a limb with both hands, he dangled for a humiliating second or two before finally relocating a supporting branch with one foot.

He could imagine Carlos and Murphy snickering behind their hands during this stellar performance. They both knew he had plenty of water in the truck. They knew because he always brought enough for all of them. Dehydration was a real danger working outside in Arizona.

But he was willing to look foolish in front of the guys and accept the bottled water from a woman he desperately wanted to meet. He would have liked to meet her when he was a little less fragrant, but he'd stand downwind of her and hope for the best.

No sense missing a golden opportunity because he was sweaty. If all went as he hoped with this woman, they might end up sweaty together, eventually. Yes, he was getting ahead of himself, but this connection had fate written all over it.

He dropped to the ground and headed toward her, ignoring his two employees. If either of them took this moment to go to his truck and pull a bottle of water out of the ice chest, they'd be on fertilizer duty for the rest of the summer.

"I didn't mean to interrupt your work." Her voice had a silky quality to it.

He liked silky. Silky usually meant a woman had a sensuous nature. "That's okay. I needed to take a break, anyway."

"I'll bet. You look hot."

So do you, sweet thing. Her eyes were a startling shade of blue, possibly helped along by tinted contacts. He liked the blue, although he wondered what color her eyes were, really. "But it's a dry heat."

"Yeah, right." She laughed and held out the dripping bottle. "Here. This should help."

"You're a lifesaver." He took the bottle, his hand brushing hers. He figured that was the idea. She'd obviously brought the water so they could have an interchange. As a way to meet a guy, it was clever.

"That's me," she said. "Kasey Lifesaver."

"Kasey?" He unscrewed the top of the bottle. "Is that all one word or initials?"

"One word. *K-a-s-e-y*. Kasey."

"Nice to meet you Ms. Kasey Lifesaver. I'm Sam Grateful." He took a long drink of the water, gulping down half the bottle. Although he really was thirsty, the drinking moment gave him time to think. He'd ask her to dinner. Yeah, that was a good idea. Dinner. What about tonight? Did he have anything going?

Damn it, he did. The Tin Tarantulas had a gig in a little club downtown, and he'd promised to be there. He didn't think taking a woman to hear his brother's very loud rock band was right for a first date. So he'd ask for tomorrow night, although he hated to wait that long.

He took one last swallow, lowered the bottle and smiled at her. "Thanks. That was great."

"You're welcome."

"Listen, in exchange for the water, how about if I—"

"So how come you climb around in the tree? Wouldn't it be safer to use one of those cherry-picker things?"

Obviously he hadn't impressed her with his coordination. "You mean because I almost took a header a minute ago? Usually I'm smoother than that."

"You did give me a scare, but that isn't what I meant. It seems dangerous to me, being up in the tree with a chain saw."

"Well, I'm a professional." That sounded stuffy, so he grinned and added, "Don't try this at home."

"Don't worry about that! Just watching you makes me nervous."

"Don't be. I've logged a lot of hours in plenty of trees." But her comment made him realize she probably worked in the office next to this tree and had been observing him from her window. That was gratifying. "I do use a cherry picker for some jobs, like palms and eucalyptus, but for big mesquites like this with an elaborate canopy, I'd rather get right into the tree so I can see how it needs to be shaped."

"Oh." She glanced over at the mesquite. "I guess there's more to it than I thought."

"Believe me, there's more to it than I thought when I first started out." He didn't want to talk about his work, though. He wanted to ease back around to the subject of having dinner tomorrow night. "Listen, would you—"

"Are you by any chance free for dinner tonight?"

Oh, hell. Now she'd beaten him to it. "Not tonight, but tomorrow night, I'd love to."

She hesitated. "Well, tomorrow night I have this...thing. Maybe the next night...no, wait a minute, there's—"

"Hold on." He could see they were losing steam, and

he didn't want that. "Let me tell you what I have to do tonight. You might be willing to go with me."

"Okay." She looked wary. "What is it?"

"My little brother has this rock band, and they're playing tonight at the Cactus Club. It's not exactly my kind of music—they appeal to a younger crowd, but this is an important gig, and I want to show my support, so I promised I'd be there."

Instead of making a face, she actually looked interested. "What's the name of the band?"

"The Tin Tarantulas. I'm sure you've never heard of them."

"But I have! I heard them play when I was...um, when I just happened to be down at ASU last year. It was an open-air kind of performance. I...the college kids really seemed to love their music." She combed her hair back with both hands, a gesture that jiggled her breasts under the lacy top. "I wouldn't mind going, if that's your question."

"It's my question." He was careful not to let his gaze rest where it wanted to and looked into her eyes, instead. "So that wouldn't be too painful? We can have dinner first, of course, but I need to be at the Cactus Club by nine. Colin expects me to show up."

"That'll work." She smiled. "And don't forget I asked you to dinner, so that part's on me."

"Okay." He was so wrapped up in her smile that he didn't care to debate who would pick up the check. Her lips, decorated in the same shade of red as her car, made him think of hot kisses. But what made her mouth even more fascinating to him, a man who loved details, was the tiny scar in one corner.

It was so faint that someone would have to look close to notice, but that little scar made her unique, and he liked that. Maybe tonight he'd ask her how she got it. He loved hearing those kinds of stories about people. It gave him a handle on who they were.

"How about if I pick you up around seven?" she asked.

He thought about that and laughed. "That's okay. I'll drive. I'd probably need a shoehorn to get myself into your car."

She gazed at him. "How do you know that?"

Uh-oh. Oh, well. Confession was good for the soul. "I saw you get out of your car this morning."

"Really?" The light dawned. "Were you the person who honked?"

"I accidentally hit the horn." *Leaning forward to get a better view of your tush.* "Sorry if I startled you."

"I just thought somebody was trying to get my attention. But when no one called out my name, I figured it wasn't for me."

It was all for her, but he'd eat grubs before admitting that. "I didn't know your name then." He laughed. "I still only know half of it, Ms. Lifesaver."

She held out her hand. "Kasey Braddock."

He wiped his on his jeans. "Sam Ashton." He noted that her handshake was firm and her skin felt cool and incredibly soft. She met his gaze during the brief moment of touching, and he enjoyed the warmth of their eye contact.

What a great custom, the handshake. Sam thought of it as a sample of who the person was, like a taste of an ice-cream flavor served on a tiny pink spoon. In this instance, the sample made him want to take home a gallon's worth of Kasey Braddock.

KASEY WAS CONVINCED that Sam had no clue they'd ever met. After she gave him her full name and he didn't react, she knew she was home free. Of course, she hadn't expected him to react. He'd remember a buddy named Jim Winston, but the last name of Braddock shouldn't ring any bells for him.

"So I'll pick you up, then," he said.

Kasey hesitated, wondering if an assertive woman would insist on doing the driving, even if her car was a tight fit for her date. No, she'd let him drive. She knew the Miata was small, and Sam wasn't.

"Or maybe you'd rather meet at the restaurant," he said, obviously misinterpreting her reluctance. "After all, you don't really know me, so maybe you'd rather not give out your address to a perfect stranger."

But she did know him. Still, she couldn't say that. "You're Sam Ashton, so either this is your business or you're working for a relative."

"It's my business."

She'd thought as much from the way he'd talked about his work with the tree. "Then I can't believe you'd jeopardize your professional reputation by turning into some kind of stalker. I'd be glad to have you pick me up."

He smiled. "I promise I won't bring a truck."

"I'm not a car snob. You could bring a truck."

"Glad to hear it, but I'll bring my car, anyway. So let's head over to the truck and I'll locate a pen and paper."

"Okay." She walked beside him to the truck and trailer parked in the street next to the building, with orange cones set around it to divert traffic. Now she could see it was the same truck that had been parked behind her this morning. She liked knowing that he'd watched her get out of her car.

He opened the passenger door, grabbed a clipboard and closed the door again, but not before she noticed a cooler on the floor of the cab.

"Um, what's in the cooler?" she asked, thinking she already knew the answer.

He grinned sheepishly. "Bottles of water."

"I see."

"I couldn't very well tell you I didn't need that water after you'd gone to so much trouble, could I?"

"You could have." But knowing that he'd wanted to take the excuse to talk to her did a lot to calm her nerves. Maybe she was better at snagging a guy's attention than she'd thought. "But I'm glad you didn't."

"Me, too."

After giving him her phone number and address, she decided to get the heck out of there before she screwed something up. So far, so good, but her luck might not hold much longer. "See you at seven, then," she said.

"Absolutely."

She turned and walked toward the building, wondering if he was watching her. She did her damned best to walk like an experienced temptress. And she was well on her way to becoming one after successfully completing Phase One of the operation. Maybe her little red car had something to do with it, if he'd taken the time to notice her in the parking lot this morning. She thought of her license plate and wondered if he'd seen that, too.

The members of her family, especially her brother Jim, were not fans of that license plate. They'd predicted it would get her into trouble. No doubt they also wondered if that was exactly what she'd intended.

Her sexual experience so far couldn't be classified as getting into trouble. Losing her virginity in college—to another nerd—had been more of a social experiment than a night of grand passion. About a year and a half ago, she'd decided she needed a makeover to attract sexier dates, and Alicia had been there to help.

Coincidentally, her parents had sold the house she'd grown up in and moved to a condo in Gilbert, a good hour away. That small degree of separation had given her a surprising sense of freedom and had made changing her image even easier. By the time she'd started work at Beckworth Public Relations, she'd been transformed into glam girl.

To give her confidence a boost, she'd ordered the vanity plate. She'd told herself that any day now she'd start getting into that trouble her family was so worried about. Well, apparently she was going to start with Sam.

SEVERAL HOURS LATER, while dressing for her date, Kasey mulled over her game plan. After reading a ton of restaurant reviews online and interviewing her coworkers, she'd made reservations at a trendy Italian restaurant within walking distance of the Cactus Club. That way, Sam wouldn't have to worry about finding a downtown parking place twice.

Thank God she had fake ID. She'd felt like a criminal getting one in college, but it had come in handy. It would come in handy again tonight, because she wouldn't be allowed into the Cactus Club without it.

The trick to this evening, Kasey decided, was coaxing Sam to talk about himself. The less he knew about her, the less likely he'd figure out who she was, which could cause complications. Blowing her cover at work was only part of the problem. She didn't relish having Sam contact her brother, who would then fill him in on what his baby sister had been up to or, rather, *hadn't* been up to.

Therefore she wouldn't take this charade too far, only far enough to convince herself that Sam wanted her. This was simply a test of her abilities, one that would erase any lingering feelings of nerdiness she carried around and establish her new babe status for good.

At that point, she'd be ready to enjoy what the world of dating had to offer, maybe even juggling more than one guy at a time. Chances were that Sam, at age thirty, had moved beyond that exploratory stage. She'd seen the change in her brother, who'd been really serious about Alicia and hadn't dated anyone else since the breakup.

As for her, she had no illusions about holding on to Sam and zero interest in lasting relationships. She was only twenty, for crying out loud. No way would she tie herself down until she was really old, as old as her brother. As old as Sam. With tons of sexual experience.

Wiggling into the red slip dress she'd chosen for the evening, she thought about how much experience Sam must have had. A guy who looked like him must have gone horizontal with a bunch of women. She wondered what kind of lover he was.

A picture flashed through her mind—Sam sitting in the emergency room with her, Jim and her mom. Sam, looking remorseful every time he glanced her way. She'd tried to tell him it wasn't his fault, but talking made her mouth bleed, so she'd had to sit there silently and let him suffer. He'd bought her a can of root beer from the pop machine and rounded up a straw so she could drink it without moving her lips.

And then he'd sent the flowers the next day, pink, red and white carnations mixed in with baby's breath and lacy ferns. She knew now that it hadn't been an expensive bouquet, but because it was her first ever, she'd never forgotten how it had looked or how amazed she'd been when her mother had called her to the door to sign for the delivery. Come to think of it, the vase, her only one, was tucked into a cupboard in her apartment kitchen. She'd taken it when she'd moved away from home.

If he'd been that sweet at eighteen, he could be a wonderful lover with all the experience he'd surely collected since then. But she wouldn't be finding out. Way too risky. Once she'd made him drool, she was outta there and on to her regularly scheduled dating program.

She thought her outfit would be a good start. Alicia would approve of the slip dress, the high-heeled slides, the braided leather jewelry and the upswept hairdo. Sam would never connect her with the kid he'd wrestled with in the pool all those years ago.

Pacing her apartment, she reminded herself that she couldn't be too enthusiastic about the Tin Tarantulas, either. Even though she'd loved their music the one time she'd heard them play, they definitely appealed to the college crowd more than young professionals. And she was a young professional now. She should act slightly bored.

Maybe she needed to practice her slightly bored expression. After returning to her bathroom, she stood in front of the mirror and tried out a sigh and an upward roll of her eyes. Yeah, that was good. A world-weary, tolerant smile, perhaps. Excellent.

Her doorbell rang, and she yelped softly. World-weary disappeared as her heart pumped faster and her palms grew sweaty. Sam Ashton had arrived to take her out for the evening. How amazing was that?

She dried her shaking hands on a towel, took one last glance at her flushed cheeks, and decided she'd have to work on her bored expression later. Right now she looked and felt exactly like that little kid who'd received her first bouquet of flowers twelve years ago.

3

SAM STOOD at Kasey's door holding a dozen first-cut red roses in a cone of green tissue paper. In his early and poor-guy dating years he'd gone for the bargain roses, not understanding that those had been trimmed at least three times and wouldn't last more than a few days. First-cut lasted much longer, long enough to make a real impression.

That's what Sam intended to do. He had a gut feeling about this woman. Although he'd be hard-pressed to explain why she seemed so right for him, he was letting his instincts dictate his actions. Thus the pricey roses on the first date. He wanted to let her know he wasn't kidding around.

When she opened the door and he got a look at her red slip dress and take-me-now shoes, he was doubly glad he'd brought the first-class roses. A woman who looked like Kasey Braddock had seen her share of bouquets, and he wanted his to stand out from the crowd.

"Hi," she said. "Wow, roses."

"And I'm sure glad I picked red." He handed her the bouquet. If she was used to getting flowers, she didn't let on. "I'm guessing it's your favorite color."

"It's my new favorite color. Come in and I'll find a vase for these."

"It should be your favorite color." He stepped inside the door. "You look terrific in it."

"Thanks." She gave him a quick smile. "Have a seat. I'll be back in a sec."

He nodded, although he had no intention of sitting down. He'd be able to get a better view of her apartment if he stood right where he was.

What he saw surprised him a little. It looked like a college pad instead of a career girl's place. Makeshift bookcases of bricks and boards overflowed with paperbacks, hardbacks and what looked like textbooks. A futon took the place of a regular couch, and over it hung posters from various art galleries. The women he'd dated recently had graduated to real furniture and professionally framed prints.

The place was neat enough, but it didn't look as if she'd spent lots of time thinking about decorating. One scraggly pothos in dire need of repotting hung from a hook in the ceiling, and the coffee table looked like a hand-me-down from her parents.

Okay, so she wasn't domestic, wasn't into nest-building. Was that such a problem? Reluctantly he admitted it might be. Nest-building instincts ranked pretty high on his list these days.

Then she walked back into the room holding the flowers, her cheeks flushed and the rosebuds a perfect match for her lipstick, and he forgot about his nest-building requirements. Hell, if this turned into something wonderful, he could build the damned nest. Roles were changing more every day. So what if she didn't own a decent crystal vase and had plunked his roses in a cheap glass one that looked like it had been stashed in a cupboard for years.

"Thank you for the flowers. They're gorgeous." From her expression, anyone would think he'd given her diamonds.

He found her enthusiasm sexy. Maybe she didn't bother decorating her apartment or buying crystal because she had too many other exciting things in her life, like asking a complete stranger to have dinner with her.

"Okay." She set the vase of flowers on the coffee table and scooped up a small purse from the futon. "I'm ready."

He thought of her license plate. Yep, her vibrant approach to life really turned him on. "Then let's go."

HALFWAY THROUGH THE MEAL, Kasey congratulated herself on how well she was doing. Probably because the restaurant was upscale, the waiter hadn't carded her when Sam had ordered a bottle of red to go with the pasta. She was relieved about that. Although she had the fake ID, she didn't want to use it more than necessary, in case somebody spotted it as bogus.

As per her plan, she'd steered the conversation so they talked about Sam. During the antipasto, she'd confirmed what she already knew, that his family had moved to Oregon right after his senior year in high school. He'd gone to college up there but never could get used to the weather, so he'd decided to come back to Phoenix to build his landscaping business.

With a little prompting, she got him to talk about his business during the main course. She didn't blame him for being proud of what he'd accomplished, creating a thriving enterprise during tough economic times. Besides, she liked listening to him. There was a sexy, husky sound to his voice that hadn't been there when he was eighteen.

"The tree you worked on today looks amazing," she said. "Like a sculpture. How did you learn to do that?"

He put down his wineglass and gazed across the table at her, a little smile on his face. "Oh, I've had a lot of practice. Besides, it's fun. I like climbing trees. It's probably not much different from you designing a PR campaign. How do you go about that, by the way?"

Although it was an innocent enough question, she pegged it as an attempt to switch the topic to her. "Trust me, it's not half as interesting as what you do. So, what's the biggest landscaping challenge you've ever had?"

He grinned at her. "I'm beginning to think you've dated a bunch of egomaniacs."

"Why?"

"Oh, just the way you've made sure we talked about me all the time. Maybe the other guys wanted to bask in that constant limelight, but I'd love to hear something about you."

"I'm... I'm not all that fascinating." It was a truthful statement. She was hoping to *become* fascinating, but that would require more seasoning. He was to be part of the process, although he didn't know that.

"Come on. A woman who drives a red convertible with such an interesting license plate?"

So here was the fatal flaw in her plan. With the car, the dress, even the shoes, she'd presented herself as a daring *Sex and the City* kind of girl. She'd hoped that concentrating on him would prevent the spotlight from being turned on her. Spotlights picked up discrepancies. She wondered what she could offer up that would fit the image she'd projected without telling him too much.

Then she remembered her current project at work. "Well, right now I'm designing an image make over for Slightly Scandalous."

His eyebrows rose. *"Really."*

"So you know the place?"

"Um, yeah, I've heard of it."

From his initial reaction she thought he'd had more intimate contact than that. At any rate, sexy underwear seemed to be a savvy topic that went with the red car and the license plate. She'd get some mileage out of it.

"They've seen how well Victoria's Secret is doing," she said, "and they want some of that market. They've rented mall space and they want a classier image when they move."

"So how do you do that? I mean, when I think of Slightly Scandalous, I think of G-strings and those bras with the cutouts...everywhere."

Having him mention such things changed the atmosphere of the table, and maybe that's what she needed. She wouldn't get him to drool over a discussion about trimming trees. "Exactly. It's all about branding. If I do my job right, when you think of Slightly Scandalous, you'll picture a runway model in silk underwear that's decent enough to be shown on national TV and yet still very sexy."

"So they're giving up on the other stuff?" He sounded disappointed.

"Pretty much. There's a niche market for the over-the-top lingerie, but apparently they were struggling to capture that." She decided a happening chick would be bold. "Face it, did you ever go in there?"

A flush stole up from the open collar of his silk shirt. "Maybe I should plead the Fifth on that one."

Which meant he had bought naughty lingerie at some time, for some woman in his life. Kasey wondered what that would be like, having a man like Sam bring her a present of underwear that he expected her to model for him. The idea gave her goose bumps.

"I have the feeling I've just incriminated myself," he said.

"Not at all." But he'd made himself seem even sexier, if that was possible. She reminded herself to keep playing the role of sophisticated city girl. "I know men have fantasies."

His gaze intensified. "I've been told women have them, too."

"Well, of course." She sounded nervous, damn it. She decided to retreat a little. "That's what my project's about, tapping into women's fantasies instead of catering to a man's. Women usually want their fantasies packaged more subtly."

"How about you? How do you like your fantasies packaged?"

I'm looking at it. "Oh, I'm probably like most women."

"I seriously doubt that. Play fair, now. I've pretty much admitted to buying something at Slightly Scandalous. The least you can do is confess that you've worn something from there."

As if. "Uh, well, I—"

"Your pink cheeks are giving you away, Kasey." He smiled. "I know a bad girl when I see one. But for the record, wearing an outfit from Slightly Scandalous is okay with me."

She knew she was in over her head. But the thing was, she'd nearly accomplished her mission. Sam looked like a man who could hardly wait to get her alone.

Picking up her goblet, she borrowed his line. "I'll have to take the Fifth on that." Then she drained the glass before setting it back on the table.

He let out a breath. "You know how to turn a man inside out, don't you?" He picked up the wine bottle and refilled her glass.

She made a command decision not to drink another drop. Finishing off her glass had seemed like a big-girl sort of gesture, but now she was feeling light-headed and giggly. Any more of that delicious red stuff and she was liable to tell Sam her entire life story. Nope, she'd stick with water from here on out.

In fact, a drink of water might settle her jumpy nerves. The way Sam was looking at her, she had the feeling she'd started something she might not be ready to finish. She picked up her water glass and took a cooling swallow.

"I've been dying to ask you—how did you get that little scar on your lip?"

She choked on the water. As an unplanned distraction, it worked well. Sam was out of his seat in no time, patting her back and murmuring words of concern.

Gradually she could breathe again, and she begged him to go back to his seat. Other diners had begun to stare and even the waiter had come by to make sure she was all right.

Sam eased back into his chair. "Sure you're okay?"

"Fine. Just embarrassed. You'd think by now I'd have learned how to swallow water."

"I hope it wasn't something I said."

"No, no, nothing like that."

"If mentioning that little scar upset you, I'm really sorry."

"Goodness, no. It's an old childhood injury. Most of the time I forget it's even there." She'd always cherished that scar, though, because it reminded her of Sam. He really had been her fantasy guy for years. That was one negative thing about running into him again. Chances were he wouldn't be able to live up to the image she'd created for him.

"I'll bet you were goofing around on the playground equipment," he said.

"Something like that." And they needed to get off this subject before she let some detail slip.

"I remember wrestling with my buddy's kid sister years ago in their swimming pool. I got too rough and she ended up needing stitches. I felt like a jerk."

She had to work very hard not to react. "You shouldn't have. I'm sure it wasn't intentional."

"Yeah, but I should have been more careful. She was just a kid—only about seven or eight. I can't even remember her name, but I can still see that little face, with an ice pack crammed against her mouth."

"I'm sure she recovered." *Although she missed you dreadfully and carried you in her heart for years.*

"Oh, I'm sure she did, too. I checked with my buddy after a couple of months, to make sure. But then he went into the service and we lost track of each other. I haven't tried to find him since I got back. I should. Maybe that's why we're having this conversation, to remind me to look up my old buddy Jim and see if he's back in town."

And Kasey couldn't stop him from doing that, either. One evening with Jim could be enough to blow her cover. She might as well enjoy this date with Sam, because there was a good chance she'd never have another one.

By THE END OF THE MEAL, Sam hadn't made much progress in getting to know Kasey. And he wanted to get to know her, because physically she was driving him crazy. In the old days he would have given in to that physical urge and figured that he'd get around to the friendship part later. Now that seemed backward to him. He wanted to establish a relationship first.

Kasey wasn't helping. Being a mystery woman seemed to appeal to her, and that attitude had one-night stand written all over it. Maybe that's what she had in mind. After all, she'd made the first move and she'd insisted on paying for dinner. He'd tried to get the check, but she'd outmaneuvered him.

So maybe he was designated as her boy-toy for the night. He wasn't about to fall in with that plan. Of course he wasn't. Not even if he did find himself staring at her mouth and longing to stare at her cleavage.

He wanted to touch her...all over. As they left the restaurant, he settled for holding her hand. Even that simple contact aroused him. He should be offended at the idea that she might want him just for sex and nothing more. Instead he was challenged by it.

Unfortunately, the next part of the evening wouldn't allow much conversation between them. He had about three blocks before they'd be drawn into the noisy world of the Cactus Club. After that, they'd have to read lips.

"Do your folks live in Phoenix?" he asked, trying yet again.

"Uh, no. Gilbert."

"That area sure is growing. Is that where you went to school?"

"Not exactly. Whoops, the light's about to change. We'll have to hurry to make it." She tugged at his hand.

He resisted. "Maybe I don't care."

"Oh." She gave him a wary glance. "All right. We can wait until the light changes."

He decided the time had come for some gentle persuasion. Taking her other hand, he pulled her closer. "Kasey, why are you hiding from me?"

She laughed. "Hiding? Why would you say that?"

"Because every time I try to learn something about you, you find a way to avoid answering." He released his grip on her hands and cupped her shoulders. What silky skin she had. "I want to get to know you." He wondered if he was imagining the quick look of panic in her eyes.

Then it was gone, and she smiled. "In what way?"

In every way. "You know—the kinds of things you liked to do as a kid, the type of music you like, whether you have a favorite team or hate sports altogether."

"I like baseball, and my favorite team is the Diamondbacks."

"Me, too." But out of all the things he'd asked, she'd picked the least personal one to answer. Most everyone in Phoenix liked the home team. Nevertheless, although he really knew nothing more than he had before, he found himself caressing her shoulders and wanting to kiss her. Theoretically, he shouldn't get involved in a kiss with a woman who held her cards so close to her chest.

But what a chest it was, and he longed to know how it felt locked against his. "Okay, that's a start." He drew her closer. "How about music?"

"I like everything."

"Everything?" He couldn't take his gaze from her mouth. So tempting. "Even rap?"

"Some rap is okay."

He loved the way her lips rounded as she said the *o* in *okay.* "Can you sing?" It was a goofy question, but he was so focused on her mouth it seemed semilogical.

"Not very well." She looked up at him. "Can you?"

"Not very well." Then temptation overtook him. Forgetting why he didn't want to do this yet, he leaned down and kissed her.

And what a mistake that was, because she kissed him back. She might not want to tell him anything about herself, but she was perfectly willing to kiss him as if the end of the world had arrived. Her lips parted, her tongue became involved, and when he wrapped his arms around her and pulled her close, she settled against him with a soft moan of delight.

As kisses went, this one topped the charts. He tasted hunger as strong as his own, which filled his mind with all sorts of ideas he wasn't supposed to be having. In fact, much more of this kiss and they were liable to get themselves arrested. He pulled back with difficulty and looked into her eyes to double-check that he hadn't misread her level of involvement. Yep—eyes glazed, chest heaving, body quivering. Just like his.

"I...had a feeling about this," he said.

"N-not me."

"Boy, I did. Sometimes there's just...something between two people." Now there was a profound statement. Sheesh. He rubbed his hands up and down her arms, as if trying to restore the circulation, which was ridiculous. Judging from her reaction, her circulation was currently excellent. Speaking for himself, he could feel the blood whipping through his veins and arteries at warp speed.

"Something explosive." She still sounded out of breath.

"Right. But I believe in getting to know each other first."

She cleared her throat. "Okay."

"Unfortunately, going to my little brother's event won't give us much chance for that. The noise level will be horrific. And I can't leave too early or he'll think I didn't like it."

"Then we need to go and stay as long as necessary."

"I'm afraid so. But after that..." He didn't dare put

what he was thinking into words. He hoped she was thinking exactly the same thing.

"After that, we'll...we'll see what happens."

So she wanted to hedge a little. He didn't buy her act. He'd been there during the fireworks and he knew she was flammable. "I think we both can guess what will happen, given half a chance."

"I thought you wanted to get to know me first."

"I do." He gave her a quick, hard kiss. "And I will."

4

SOMEHOW KASEY CROSSED the street without getting run over. That probably had something to do with Sam's tight grip on her hand and his take-charge attitude. Thank goodness he was watching out for them, because she was too dazed by that kiss to notice traffic signals.

So when had kissing become such a big deal? She'd kissed guys before and been able to analyze the process in clinical detail, even during the act itself. She'd evaluated kissing techniques and rated them for firmness, taste and the all-important slipperiness factor. Then she'd taken into account the groping, or lack of groping, and whether that added to the experience or detracted.

Then along came Sam with a kiss that destroyed every analytical brain cell she possessed. Instead of being a mildly amusing mouth exercise, this kiss had thrown her into the center of a tornado where she'd clung helplessly to Sam as winds of lust tugged at her from every angle. Whatever he was offering, she wanted to be first in line.

All her sexual experiences so far had been motivated by curiosity. This driving urge was nothing like that. There was desperation mixed in with carnal desire, as if she might go crazy if she couldn't satisfy the need he'd created with one simple kiss. No, not *simple*. That had been a very complicated kiss. Because of it, she had to reevaluate her entire campaign.

Her original plan had included more control. She'd judged her ability to stay in control based on her experiences with men so far. She hadn't factored in a kiss that would turn her knees to jelly. She'd always thought that was a silly expression, someone's wild exaggeration of normal sexual impulses.

Apparently not. Apparently there were men like Sam who could accomplish the knees-to-jelly thing. Who knew? In any case, she had a combustible situation on her hands. He wanted to sleep with her. That was the good part, because she really had made him drool. The bad part was that she wanted to sleep with him, too.

So now what? A big juicy flirtation was what she'd intended. A full-blown affair hadn't been part of the equation. Obviously that's what he wanted, though.

And so did she, but it wouldn't be a wise move. In fact, it would be an extremely foolish move. The deeper her involvement, the more likely he'd find out who she was. She didn't want that to happen.

Instead, she wanted to be the sexy mystery woman who got away. She might still be able to pull that off, but she'd have to keep her wits about her. No more of those high-octane kisses. And this would be their one and only date.

By the time she'd reached that conclusion, Sam had opened the door to the Cactus Club. A warm-up band had already taken the stage and the air vibrated with the sound of drums and acoustic guitars.

Kasey dug into her small purse and pulled out her fake ID. Showing it always made her nervous, but tonight provided a double dose of angst. Nothing could be more embarrassing than getting busted in front of Sam. Fortunately the interior was dim, the guy checking ID knew Sam, and there was no special scrutiny of her card.

"Colin's saved you a table up front," the guy said, leaning close to be heard above the music. "He also said the first round's on him."

"We'll see about that," Sam said with a smile. Then he guided Kasey to an empty table right next to the crowded dance floor.

Once there, he held her chair and leaned down to speak directly into her ear. "What do you want to drink?"

She turned to answer him and her mouth nearly collided with his. When she pulled back, he caught her chin with his hand.

"Hey, there." He stayed in close, a gentle smile on his face. "You're not having a shyness attack, are you?"

Shy was the last word she wanted him to associate with her. "Not in the least." She smiled back. "But I didn't want to be the cause of you getting teased, in case your brother's around."

"Let me worry about that." His expression grew warmer and he stroked her chin with his thumb. "I sure wish we didn't have to be here."

"But we do."

"Yeah. So what do you want?"

She'd watched enough movies and read enough

books to know that a happening chick would pick up on that opening. "Whatever you're offering, Sam."

He groaned. "Later. Later you can have whatever you want. Right now all I can give you is a drink."

"Mineral water, then."

His smile widened. "I like that. A woman who wants to stay alert. I think I'll have the same."

"Don't abstain on my account."

"Oh, it's completely on your account. Normally I enjoy the band much more when I'm a little sloshed. But for tonight, I'll forgo that crutch."

"For heaven's sake, at least have a beer."

"Nope." He shook his head. "Considering what's at stake later on, this will be no sacrifice."

Her heart beat like crazy as she absorbed his meaning. If only she could go with the flow, but she didn't dare, not with this man. "You seem to have forgotten about getting acquainted first."

"No, I haven't." He dropped a slow, lingering kiss on her lips.

She couldn't stop him without making a scene. And from that first magic taste, she didn't want to stop him. Once again, she was lost to the world. The music faded and the crowd noise disappeared. There was only the sweet pressure of his mouth on hers, and she wanted more, so much more....

He ended the kiss and took a shaky breath. "There."

She opened her eyes, feeling like Sleeping Beauty. But this was no fairy tale and she was not going to be swept away by the handsome prince. Not if she could help it.

"I know you better already," he murmured.

"You can't find out anything from a kiss."

"Sure I can. For example—"

"Can I take your order, sir?" called out a waiter who'd appeared behind Sam.

Kasey glanced over Sam's shoulder and caught the waiter's eye. He winked at her. Being with Sam had already elevated her status. No waiter had ever winked at her before.

Sam straightened and turned around. As he gave the guy their order, Kasey took a moment to dredge up some of her famous self-discipline. She hadn't graduated from college at eighteen by allowing distractions to ruin her game plan. This was no different. Well, it was a little bit different. Okay, it was a *lot* different.

But if she'd been disciplined in her studies, she could be disciplined in limiting the amount of kisses that went on. No, not limiting—eliminating. She couldn't afford any more moments of oblivion. She quickly reviewed her list of reasons and vowed to keep them firmly in mind.

Sam took his seat across from her and plopped the waiter's ordering pad on the small table.

She raised her voice to make herself heard. "What are you doing with that?"

"Borrowed it for a while!" He scribbled something on the pad, tore off the top sheet and handed it across the table, along with the pen he'd apparently scrounged from the waiter.

She glanced at the paper, where he'd written, "Are you a morning person or a night person?" She started to laugh. No wonder he'd built a successful business. He was an extremely resourceful guy. She admired that in people, and she was gradually coming to admire Sam, not to mention wanting to jump his bones.

After writing "night person" on the paper, she handed it back. That kind of information shouldn't get her in trouble. Mainly she had to avoid biographical information like where she went to high school, which was also his high school.

Sam wrote "me, too" under her answer and held it up so she could see it. He seemed pleased to have that in common, but then he probably expected this was the start of something spectacular. She was starting to feel guilty, because it wouldn't be the start of anything. Unfortunately, she thought of him as sexual training wheels, and that wasn't fair to him or any guy. Maybe she should give some excuse about hating the music and make her exit.

She didn't need to hang around any more to see she had temptress potential or even to have stories for the women at the office. Her goal of making him want her had been accomplished and then some. She'd earned her first stripe as a Bad Girl, so she could stop the charade now.

He would be hurt and confused, would probably try to contact her again, but she could handle that. What she couldn't handle was getting in deeper with him and then forcing herself to back away. Right now she'd inflict only superficial wounds on his ego, but the longer she played this game, the worse it would be on him.

Meanwhile Sam was busy writing another question. He pushed the paper across the table and tossed her the pen.

This was her chance to leave. All she had to do was flip the page over and write "Have to go—music's giving me a headache." He wouldn't be able to leave with her, not when his brother's band was about to take the stage. He'd probably call her a cab, and that would be that.

If she meant to leave, she shouldn't read whatever question he'd come up with, because the question wouldn't matter. But she'd been born with an extremely inquisitive mind. The trait had been a blessing for the most part, but was a curse, now.

Chastising herself for doing it, she read his question. "What was your favorite book when you were seven years old?" Damn it, she knew she shouldn't have read his question. He wasn't just playing at this get-acquainted business. He really wanted to know who she was. Okay, she'd answer his question, and maybe that would send him running for the hills.

She picked up the pen and wrote "*Megatrends for Women*. Yours?" Then she scooted the paper across the table and waited for his reaction, the reaction she usually got from all except the genius-level guys.

Sure enough, his eyes widened and he glanced up. She could almost read his thoughts—*system alert: brainiac in the house.* Then he smiled and picked up the pen. He continued to smile as he wrote down his favorite book and added another line, maybe another question.

When he pushed the paper over to her, she hesitated before picking it up. She was supposed to be out of here by now. Instead she was still trading notes with Sam. But she had to find out what he'd written, and what his next question would be. Without realizing it, he'd chosen a method of communication that tapped right into her curious nature. She found the suspense contained in each note irresistible.

Glancing down, she read "*Goodnight, Moon* was my favorite book. I think you're probably a lot smarter than I am. Is that a problem for you?" She looked up and saw the uncertainty in his expression. He wasn't rejecting her because of her brains—he was afraid she'd reject him.

Her heart turned over. She couldn't leave now. Instead she wrote "No way" across the bottom of the page and gave it back to him.

His face relaxed into another broad smile and he flipped the paper over to write something across the back. This time he didn't give her the pen, only the small sheet of paper.

When she read what he'd written, her pulse rate jumped. "I promise to compensate in other areas." Sweet heaven, the man was ready to guarantee that he'd love her so well she wouldn't care about his IQ.

THE TIN TARANTULAS' opening number put an end to the note writing for a while, but that was okay with Sam. Thanks to that maneuver, he was getting a handle on Kasey Braddock. What he'd taken as a standoffish attitude might be related to her heavy-duty smarts.

She hadn't wanted him to know she was a brain. Understandable. He wasn't oblivious to the problems that could have caused with the opposite sex once she started dating. Some guys reacted poorly if they found out a woman was more intelligent than they were.

Sam happened to think it was cool. He liked hanging

out with smart people. He'd discovered that early in his life during interactions with Colin, who had inherited more brains than he had. When discussing things with Colin, he sometimes lost his way in the conversation, but he was never bored. So if Kasey didn't mind the gap in mental abilities, he sure as hell didn't.

Good thing he'd thought up the note idea, or he might never have found out her secret. She must have decided to test him when he asked about her favorite book as a kid. Maybe she'd thought that would be the end of the attraction for him.

It was far from the end. This woman had beauty *and* brains. What a combo. He'd also decided something else about Kasey. She wasn't nearly as sophisticated as she wanted everyone to believe.

He wondered if she'd gone through school as a nerd, then transformed herself when she got into the working world. Tinted contacts, a different hairstyle, a new wardrobe, a sexy little car—they could be the props of her new image.

In the PR business, her brains wouldn't get her shunned, they'd get her promoted. In the dating game, unfortunately, there were still a lot of men who had to feel superior to woman in all ways. Kasey might have bumped up against a few of those, so she was careful how much she revealed about herself. And she might not have had the busy social life he'd imagined.

All that was good news as far as he was concerned. If she was searching for a guy who appreciated everything about her, including all that mental firepower, Sam was her man. This was turning into a very exciting evening, and it wasn't even half-over.

At one point Kasey leaned across the table to ask which member of the band was his brother, and Sam pointed him out. That reminded him that watching Colin was the reason he was here, and he needed to pay better attention. Colin played lead guitar. The band included a bass guitarist, drummer and a keyboard player who was also the vocalist.

The dress code for the Tin Tarantulas was black. Anything was acceptable if it was the color of soot. T-shirts, silk shirts, cargo pants and bell-bottoms appeared in various combinations.

Colin wore low-slung jeans and a plain black T-shirt. His long black hair flew in all directions and his gold earrings caught the light as he went wild on his electric guitar. The in-your-face musical style obviously satisfied the customers filling the tiny dance floor and crowding around the tables.

Sam hoped Kasey was tolerating it okay. At the end of the first number she applauded with such enthusiasm that he couldn't believe she was faking it. Much to his amazement, she actually seemed to like the music. That was a bonus—a surprising bonus, but a bonus nevertheless. He'd been afraid she'd be suffering through this club scene.

Instead, she tapped her feet and moved in time with the music. He was so fascinated watching her that it took a few minutes before he figured out she might want to dance. Standing, he held out his hand.

She seemed startled, and then quickly shook her head. "That's okay," she murmured. Immediately she stopped tapping her feet and twitching in response to the beat.

He leaned closer so he wouldn't have to shout. Man, did she smell good. "Oh, come on," he coaxed. "I'm no twinkle toes, myself."

"I'm definitely not a twinkle toes." She folded her hands on the table, as if that would keep her from moving with the music.

"Look, the floor's so small, all we have room to do is stand there and wiggle."

Apparently that got to her. She glanced up at him and grinned. "I'm going to risk embarrassing myself just so I can watch you do that."

"Good deal." He pulled her to her feet and they edged onto the crowded floor.

He hadn't done this kind of bump and grind in a while, so he felt a little self-conscious, but he wanted to give her every reason to let loose. That meant forgetting that his little brother was up on the stage and would no doubt comment on his dance moves at great length. Sam surrendered to that inevitability and began to shake his booty.

And praise the Lord, so did Kasey. She started out with small, tight movements, but when Sam challenged her by exaggerating his own moves, she laughed and threw herself into it. Before long she was making those gorgeous breasts of hers shimmy.

Sam wanted to stop dancing and simply watch, but then she might stop, too, and he couldn't have that. So he kept dancing and encouraging her with laughter and smiles. She was amazing. If he'd ever thought the bass was too loud, he didn't think so now. That rhythm echoed through his body and hers, linking them together in a way that was almost like sex.

He'd never danced like this in his life, not even when he was drunk. Tonight he was dancing under the influence, though—the influence of Kasey, a woman who knew how to shake his world.

5

KASEY ABANDONED her slightly bored routine. She'd loved the bold music played by the Tin Tarantulas when she'd heard them at ASU. Sitting right up front at the Cactus Club, where the beat felt like tennis balls bouncing in her veins, made her long to move with it. But she hadn't meant to dance.

Then Sam had proposed that they could stand there and wiggle, as he'd put it, and she'd been unable to resist seeing how he'd look on the dance floor. Passing up that chance might lose her the Bad Girl's stripe she'd already earned. As it turned out, Sam knew how to wiggle.

Watching him lose himself to the music tripped a switch in her, and she abandoned herself to the heavy beat. Back in school she'd danced away her stress alone in the privacy of her dorm room where no one could comment on what she looked like doing it. Tonight the combination of the dress, the shoes and Sam gave her the confidence to shake it up in public.

When no one seemed to be pointing and laughing, she let herself go a little more with each number. What fun. What a huge relief to know she could play with the big boys and girls at the nightclub.

Sam looked at her as if he'd like to find a more secluded playground for just the two of them. She didn't know how she'd deal with that hunger in his eyes, especially because dancing to the wild beat was turning her on, too. But for now she wanted to revel in the feeling that she owned this dance floor. She'd never felt that way, and it was a big step in her evolution from nerd-girl to hot babe.

They danced until the band took a break, then collapsed into their seats, panting. Taped music took over, but it wasn't nearly as loud or boisterous, so the dance floor emptied. She gave up on keeping her hair tidy and took the pins out so it fell to her shoulders.

Sam wiped his forehead with a napkin. "I'm getting too old for this."

That brought her up short. He thought he was getting too old for dancing at the Cactus Club, and she'd just found her dancing feet. She had to be realistic. No matter how wonderfully he kissed, he was too old for her, or she was too young for him, whichever way she looked at it.

But she wanted him to believe she was a contemporary, so she nodded. "I know what you mean."

He smiled at her. "I doubt it. You look fresh as a daisy. Like you can hardly wait for the band to start up again."

"I like how they play." She might as well admit that. After the way she'd reacted to their tunes, she couldn't pretend indifference now.

"And I'm glad you do!" Hair flying around his shoulders, Colin arrived. He grabbed a vacant chair, turned it backward and sat down between them. Then he stuck out his hand. "Hi, I'm Colin, the wayward little brother."

Kasey shook his hand. "Kasey Braddock. Your music's great." She figured he was in his early twenties, much closer to her age than Sam was. In theory, he'd make a more compatible date for her. When he wasn't onstage he'd be happy to dance the night away in a place like this. So why did she look at Colin and think he was way too young for her?

"Nice job, bro," Sam said. "Everyone seems to be eating this up with a spoon."

Colin beamed. "Yeah, I think they like us. Of course, all the guys made their friends come, but we counted familiar faces and only about half are people we know. The word must be getting out."

"It should," Kasey said. "I saw you when I happened to be down at ASU last year, and you gathered quite a crowd then."

"Yeah." Colin frowned. "I wish we coulda built on that, but we had some equipment problems."

Sam's jaw tightened. "Somebody swiped their amplifiers."

"And no insurance, 'cause we couldn't afford it." Colin clapped his hand on his brother's shoulder. "The big guy here saved the day and bought us new speakers, even though..." Colin paused and leaned closer to Kasey. "Don't tell anybody, but he really doesn't like our music."

"I do so like your music!" Sam looked offended. "When did I ever say I didn't?"

Colin grinned. "You don't have to say anything. It's the three beers you usually drink while we're playing that tipped me off. You aren't that much of a drinker."

He picked up the glass of mineral water in front of Sam. "What's this, straight vodka?"

Sam folded his arms over his chest. "Water. So there. I don't need three beers when I'm listening to you, obviously."

Colin took a drink. "I'll be damned. It *is* water. Maybe you need either beer or a good-looking woman to dance with." He winked at Kasey.

"Quit flirting with my date, squirt." Sam sounded like he was kidding, but his eyes said he wasn't.

"Have I ever done that?"

"Yes, you have."

"Yeah, but not seriously." He turned to Kasey. "Still, I realize it must be embarrassing to hit the dance floor with an old guy like my brother. So if you ever—"

"Hey!" Sam grabbed Colin's shoulder. He was smiling, but his grip was firm and his gaze steady. "Cut it out."

Colin laughed. "Aw, I wouldn't really try to steal her, bro. Just fooling around, teasing the big guy. Listen, I really appreciate you coming out tonight, man. And I want you to order something besides water. Seriously."

"The water was my idea," Kasey said. "Don't blame Sam. We had wine earlier, and I'm not a big drinker, either. But thanks for treating us."

"You're welcome." Colin pushed himself upright. "Wish I could do more." He glanced at Sam, his cockiness replaced by vulnerability. "So how do we sound when you're sober?"

"Amazing." Sam looked into his brother's eyes. "I'll make another contribution to the cause real soon. I have an idea for attracting more landscaping clients, and I'm considering hiring Kasey to help me grab a different part of the market. Kasey's in PR."

"Hiring me?" Kasey panicked. That wouldn't work out at all. "I'm not sure that—"

"Hey, great!" Colin returned the chair to its rightful place and leveled his gaze on his brother. "But don't go thinking you have to do this so you can give the band more money. We're okay."

"Don't worry. I'll figure out a way to make it tax deductible. You'll be doing me a favor."

Kasey scrambled for a reasonable explanation as to why she shouldn't be part of Sam's publicity scheme. "You know, I'm not very informed about landscaping."

"I could bring you up to speed," Sam said.

"Just don't do anything radical, man," Colin said. "I'm the radical one, not you. Well, I gotta head back. Nice meeting you, Kasey."

"Same here." Still trying to gather her thoughts, Kasey watched him walk away in his low-slung pants and black T-shirt. No wonder Sam wanted to help him. He was a nice kid. Then she laughed at herself for thinking that. The nice kid was probably older than she was. And Sam wanted to hire her? She had to talk him out of that.

"Just so you know, he still chews bubble gum."

She swivelled back to discover Sam looking slightly worried, as if he thought there was a chance she'd be more interested in his little brother than in him. Hardly. She'd choose Sam any day ahead of a young guy like Colin, even factoring in Sam's reluctance to spend hours on the dance floor.

But talking about Colin could buy her some time to figure out a detour around this PR idea of his. "Don't tell me you're jealous."

"Jealous? Nah. I just don't want you to act on incomplete information. He's charming and I love him, but he's a flake."

"It's obvious that you love him. He's lucky to have you." She could recommend someone else in the firm for Sam's PR needs, but then she'd still have to see him. She'd have to suggest a totally different firm.

"I can't help worrying about Colin, though." Sam took a drink of his water. "I hope to hell he makes it as a musician, because he's hopeless at a regular day job. I tried to work him into my business, but I had to let him go before he maimed himself. He was using a chain saw to play air guitar and accidentally turned the damn thing on."

"Yikes. Surely the band doesn't bring in enough to support him?"

"No. He's had a bunch of different minimum-wage jobs. He's such a fun guy that he manages to get hired, but then he starts daydreaming and screws up something or other, so he gets fired. He moved down here because he needs family around, and he couldn't stay in Oregon because Mom and Dad were always on him about the job situation. I'm kind of a nag, but not as bad as the 'rents."

"He lives with you, then?"

"Nope. He lives with a couple of band members, who don't mind if he's something of a slob." He smiled at her. "So how'm I doing? Have I managed to discourage you from going out with him?"

"I never intended to go out with him."

"The thought didn't cross your mind at all?"

She shook her head.

"He's smarter than I am."

"So what?"

"And he's absolutely right that you'd have more fun dancing with him."

"I have fun dancing with you." She gazed across the table and forgot all about the PR deal, forgot everything but Sam, the guy she'd dreamed about for twelve years. And now he wanted her enough to fight for her.

The heat generated between them was enough to melt the ice in their glasses. Kasey wondered how on earth she would get out of this evening without kissing him again. And if she gave herself that pleasure, how would she be able to deny herself the pleasures that he'd offer after that?

SAM WAS ASHAMED of himself for making Colin look bad. Although everything he'd said was true, the only reason he'd told Kasey all that was to keep her from getting interested in his little brother. And that was extremely petty. If Kasey was attracted to Colin, then that should be the end of that.

But she'd said she wasn't attracted, and from the way she was looking at him right now, he believed her. So now his conscience bothered him for saying all those things about Colin, who couldn't help being artistic and a dreamer unfit for regular work.

Sam cleared his throat. "Actually, Colin's a great

person to have around," he said. "He's funny and a lot more optimistic than I am. People really enjoy being with Colin."

"That's probably a good thing if he's going to be an entertainer. You need charisma."

"Colin has that in spades."

"You're not so bad in the charisma department, either."

"Me?" Admittedly, he felt more studly when she looked at him like that.

"Uh-huh. I—"

The band chose that moment to start up again, blasting its way into their cozy conversation, so she shrugged and smiled, obviously giving up on trying to be heard. Instead she stood and angled her head toward the dance floor, her eyebrows raised questioningly at him.

"Why not?" He pushed back his chair. A guy with charisma should be able to dance another set. He'd show Colin he wasn't over the hill, not by a long shot.

One loud, fast tune followed another, and the only thing keeping Sam upright and in motion was the sight of Kasey, who seemed perpetually ready to boogie. She had the energy of a teenager. With her skin flushed and her lipstick gone, she even looked like a teenager. She might not appreciate looking young for her age now, but someday she'd be grateful.

Sam, however, was getting tired. Just when he wondered if he would collapse in disgrace, leaving Kasey to dance without him, Colin took the microphone to announce the last number of the night. Even more surprising, he said it would be a slow tune. As Sam sighed with relief, Colin added, "So my big brother can rest up."

If Sam had the energy, he'd climb up onstage and throttle the kid. Instead he turned to Kasey and drew her into his arms. Immediately he felt his vitality returning.

Ah, she was so warm and alive, still breathing fast from all the frenzied dancing. He nestled her head against his shoulder and it fit there perfectly. Then he laid his cheek against her silky hair and breathed in her scent—shampoo and perfume blended into a sweet mixture that made him forget how tired his legs were.

The song lyrics didn't make any sense to him, but then none of the lyrics written by the Tin Tarantulas did. He didn't care, as long as he could sway on the dance floor while holding Kasey tight. He savored the pillowy softness of her breasts pressed against him and the rapid beat of her heart.

She sighed and shifted her position slightly, so that she was even more securely tucked against him. That shift was all it took to put him in arousal mode. He worked to control an impending erection and succeeded...sort of. But if she should move again...

She moved again. Her pelvis rubbed across the fly of his pants. He groaned and fought for control, wondering if she was sending him a signal or if her movements were accidental.

Might as well know. The dance floor was wall-to-wall people, with other couples locked in similar embraces, oblivious to the world. Many of the guys had already taken the kind of liberties Sam was contemplating.

Deciding to go for the gusto, he slipped both hands down Kasey's back and cupped her bottom. And did she ever have a nice one, too. She felt even better than she looked, and that was saying something.

She reacted by snuggling closer. He reacted by getting hard. She couldn't help knowing, either, so the turn of events must be A-OK with her.

The thought came to him that making love to a high-IQ woman probably wasn't much different from making love to a woman with a normal IQ. Hormones made everyone semistupid, anyway. Still, he liked the idea that she was super smart and wanted him anyway. He liked that a lot.

He thought about his house and whether he'd cleaned it up enough before he left. He thought about whether or not he'd made his bed. Then he remembered that she hadn't come across as Ms. Domesticity and that helped him relax a little.

The main thing was whether or not he'd restocked the condoms in the bedside table drawer. He probably had. Although he hadn't had sex in several months, he always lived in hope and always kept a supply of raincoats just in case.

From the feel of things, his hopes were about to be realized.

KASEY HAD NEVER DANCED this way with a man, never pressed herself against him to make absolutely certain that he was rock hard and desperate for her. But she wanted to know that about Sam, because she was quickly reaching a decision that required his complete surrender.

Maybe she wasn't thinking clearly right now. Chances were she wasn't thinking at all. How could a woman think when she was getting hot and ready for the man who currently had his hands splayed over a very tender and erotic part of her anatomy? She could feel the imprint of every finger, and whenever he gave her a squeeze, she nearly climaxed on the spot.

Yet somehow, aroused though she might be, she had to make sure her next move was the right one. Sam had thrown a monkey wrench into her plans when he'd suggested he might hire her. Yes, she could direct him to another firm... *Oh, baby, was he ever firm....*

No, she had to concentrate on this problem, on the erection...er, the direction they should take now. She sensed he might be pigheaded. And hot-blooded. *Oh, yes.* Concentrate, Kasey! He might not take direction, might not go to another company, might insist on hiring her.

But he'd take direction in bed. Mm-hmm, would he ever take direction. And she would be so glad to provide that direction. She had never in her life been so drenched in lust, and if she didn't do something about that, she might end up in the loony bin.

She could see only one way out, both to save her sanity and take care of Sam's misguided plan to hire her as a PR consultant. That way out was through Sam's bedroom. They would have sex tonight—wild, wonderful, satisfying sex. A red haze settled over her brain as she contemplated Sam, naked and willing.

She hadn't meant for tonight to end this way, but he'd given her no choice. The way she saw it—when she could think at all—having sex with him was the only answer. Once they'd spent the night writhing on his sheets, he couldn't possibly consider hiring her for PR work. And once she'd satisfied this burning desire for him tonight, she'd thank him and move on.

Technically she was turning Sam into a one-night stand. She hadn't meant to do that, but, as she'd reasoned out, it was totally his fault.

6

ONCE SHE'D REACHED her decision, Kasey focused on
making sure Sam was on board. Lifting her head from
his shoulder, she wound both arms around his neck
and gazed up at him, her eyes half-closed. Leaning
back a little allowed her hips to move forward, accen-
tuating the link between them. With the added height
of her heels she was positioned exactly right. They
could have sex against the nearest wall if everyone else
would only disappear.

With his eyes glazed and his jaw rigid, he looked like
a man ready to throw everyone else out, but she had to
be sure. Earlier he'd spent time talking about how he
needed to get to know her before sex could happen between them. She didn't want any last-minute hurdles
ruining her plan.

She moistened her lips the way she'd seen models do
on television. "Do you think you know me well
enough?"

He blinked, as if he hadn't understood the question.
"What?" His voice sounded gravelly.

"You said you wanted to get acquainted before
we..." She caressed the nape of his neck. "You know."

"Oh. Yeah. I do."

"You mean you remember you said that? Or you
think you know me well enough by now?"

"Both." He groaned softly. "You need to quit moving your hips like that."

"I'm just dancing." Yes, he was definitely on board.

"Then please stop dancing. I can't...I don't know how I'll make it back to the table."

"Or down the block to where you parked the car?" She took pity on him and just stood there.

"That, too." He sighed. "Thanks. That's a little better. Oh, hell, the music's ended, and I'm...don't go anywhere, okay?"

"I won't."

"The problem is, feeling you right there keeps me hard, but I can't let you go or everyone on the dance floor will know I'm in this condition. And my little brother's up on that stage."

"You might want to move your hands to a different location. That might help."

"Oh. Good point." He slid both hands up to rest at the small of her back. "But I'm still like a rock."

"Give yourself a minute."

"We don't have a whole lot of time before it seems kind of strange that we're still standing here."

"How have you handled this before?"

His smile was tight. "By sheer force of will. So far with you, I have zero willpower."

She realized that he was right about the time situation. They couldn't stay on the dance floor much longer. The cheers and clapping had subsided and people were returning to their tables. Soon she and Sam would look very weird standing there alone like a sculpture in the park. "Think of something else besides sex."

"I've tried. Doesn't work."

"Then I'll help. What was your worst subject in school?"

"Biology. I got sick to my stomach when we were supposed to dissect those frogs sophomore year."

"Me, too." She'd walked into the lab and walked right out again. "So how did you do in biology?"

"Almost failed the course."

She'd been able to get out of the lab work because she'd been only twelve, and the teacher had accepted a detailed report on the life of a frog instead. "So think about being in that lab, smelling the formaldehyde, picking up the scalpel, starting—"

"Yuck! Okay, you've grossed me out, and I'm much improved." Circling her waist with one arm, he turned and led her off the floor. He paused next to their table. "Hang on a minute while I leave a tip."

"I'm not going anywhere."

"Man, I hope not." He reached for his wallet, took out some bills and laid them next to his water glass. "I hope you weren't teasing me on the dance floor about wanting to continue this elsewhere."

"Nope. Not teasing."

He tucked her in next to him. "Then let's get out of here."

"You don't need to say goodbye to Colin?"

"If I know Colin, he's surrounded by admiring women and he wouldn't appreciate being interrupted while he plays rock star." Sam guided her through the tables toward the front door. "We always connect between sets. After that, we leave each other alone to do our thing."

"I see."

"And as it happens, I have something important to do."

Warmth coursed through her. "As it happens, so do I."

"That's good to hear." He gave her a squeeze. "Because your frog story is already wearing off."

THE NIGHT AIR FELT COOL against Sam's heated skin. That helped a little, but he still set a brisk pace as they covered the distance back to the car. "Am I going too fast?" he asked at one point as the staccato beat of her heels on the sidewalk made him realize she might be struggling to keep up.

"No, you're not going too fast."

Yet maybe he was, in the larger sense. This relationship had progressed to its sexual launching pad much quicker than he would have expected, but he wasn't a strong enough man to call off the countdown now. Besides, a woman as ready as Kasey seemed to be might not appreciate being left to her own devices.

He'd seen the look in her eyes out there on the dance floor. The woman needed to have someone ring her chimes, and she needed it very soon. These days ladies didn't take kindly to having a guy slow down right when they'd planned a race to the finish line.

A breeze picked up. The desert cooled off quickly after the sun went down, and the temperature could go from ninety-plus at noon to sixty at midnight. He was wearing a long-sleeved shirt, but she had no sleeves at all. "Are you warm enough?"

"Believe me, I'm plenty warm."

He chuckled and drew her tighter against his side. "I vouch for that. I'd go as far as to say you're plenty hot."

"I'd say you are, too. So don't slow down on my account, and don't worry about the temperature, either."

"Gotcha. We're making tracks." God, how he loved an eager woman. The way he was starting to see it, he and Kasey needed to get horizontal before they could make any more progress on the friendship front. Sex was getting in the way of having a decent conversation. So they'd take the edge off with a session between the sheets, and then they'd be able to talk, at long last.

He had lots he wanted to talk about, when the time came. Now that he knew she was a brain, he wanted to find out more about her childhood, which might have been way different from his. He wanted to learn about her friends, her family, her hobbies.

Besides that, he'd been serious about hiring her to do some PR. When she'd told him about changing the Slightly Scandalous store's image, it had dawned on him that he had a business that could use an image makeover. That would give him a great excuse to see her, besides potentially setting up more earning capability.

But before they could take care of business or friendship, they had to take care of pleasure. He knew sex would be fantastic with Kasey, especially if she plunged in with the same enthusiasm she'd given to dancing. Within the next hour, they would make each other very happy.

Once in his Mustang, they rode the distance to his university-area bungalow in cozy silence, holding hands across the console except when he had to shift gears. Words didn't seem necessary when they both knew exactly where they were headed and were equally interested in getting there. He didn't even bother with the radio, because the wrong song might come on and change the mood, which at the moment was perfect for what he had in mind.

The weeknight traffic was sparse, but he was careful not to speed even though he might have gotten away with it. He was taking no chances on messing this up. It could turn out to be the best sex of his entire life.

Even without speeding, he made good time to his house, an older home near ASU. "We're here," he said as he pulled into his driveway. He decided not to bother putting the car in the garage. He'd rather take her in the front door, anyway.

"You have a house?"

"The bank and I have a house. Mostly it still belongs to the bank." He'd bought the place so he could try out some landscaping ideas in the backyard, but once he'd moved in, the concept of having a serious relationship had moved right in with him.

He wondered if he'd look back on this night as the beginning of that relationship. So far, he had every reason to believe that one day he would do exactly that.

She opened her door and stepped out before he made it around to her side of the car. "A house seems so grown-up," she said.

"It has its advantages." He took her hand as they headed up a curving walkway to the door. A lamp he'd left on glowed from the living-room window. He thought it gave a welcoming look to the house, and he wanted her to feel very welcome. Extremely welcome.

"Like what advantages?"

"For one thing, no neighbors with common walls, so I can make all the noise I want." Right now he could hardly wait to get naked and vocal.

"Are you noisy?"

Heart hammering, he fit the key in the lock and turned to her. The light through the window illuminated her face. "Depends on what's happening," he said. "Are you?"

She gave him a look of pure seduction. "Depends on what's happening."

He trembled with the need to have her. "Come on." He twisted the key and shoved open the door. "Let's go in and make some noise."

KASEY HAD BEEN STARTLED to find out Sam lived in a house, much less a house he actually owned. Just when she'd decided there wasn't much of a gap between them, after all, here was more evidence that they were miles apart. She couldn't imagine renting a whole house, let alone buying one. She was years away from a step like that.

But it didn't matter, she told herself as she stepped into Sam's living room. She was here to satisfy her craving and make sure that he changed his mind about hiring her for PR work. One would take care of the other, and whether his bed was located in a rented apartment or a cute little house near the campus made no difference.

Her sexual engines had been revving ever since this date began, and she'd worked herself into a lather on the dance floor. She was completely focused on climbing into Sam's bed. Once that happened, everything else would sort itself out.

Sam seemed to be of the same mind. She had a quick glimpse of large green plants, polished wood floors and furniture slip-covered in beige. Then the front door lock clicked into place, Sam pocketed his keys and took her hand.

"This way." His tone was urgent as he led her down a darkened hallway. Then he paused and sighed. "You know, I'm acting like a sex-crazed idiot. Maybe first you'd like something to drink, a chance to tour the—"

"Later." She didn't want to give herself any more time to think about this. Right now her mind and body agreed on a course of action, and she wanted to keep it that way.

"Great." He squeezed her hand and continued down the hall to a door at the far end of the hall. Inside the room he flipped a switch and two bedside lamps came on.

He had a grown-up bed, too—king-size mattress, solid wood headboard, plaid comforter. He threw back the comforter to lay bare the creamy sheets upon which she planned to get lots of satisfaction.

Then he drew her into his arms. "We didn't have the health talk." He slipped the straps of her dress over her shoulders as he looked into her eyes. "We should probably have the health talk."

She wrapped her arms around his waist and rubbed her body against his, loving the way his eyes darkened. "Your equipment is safe with me," she murmured.

"As yours is with me." His voice was husky. "And right now, I'm really glad that I've been so damned careful all these years, because I'm free to love the living daylights out of you."

Her heart pumped wildly as she looked into his eyes. She had no doubt he was capable of doing that. "That's why I'm here."

"I know." He cupped one breast through the material of her dress. Slowly he brushed her nipple with his thumb.

She began to quiver, anticipating what lay ahead for them.

"I wanted to touch you like this on the dance floor, but I didn't dare. Dancing fast, in a dress like this, wearing no bra—you were tying me up in knots."

"Was that mean of me?" Desire thickened her tongue.

"Only if you'd told me no at the end of the night." He continued to caress her. "But you said yes. So you weren't being mean, just provocative."

She had trouble catching her breath. "I...liked the music."

"And I liked watching you like the music. To think I almost didn't take you to hear my little brother's band."

"But you did."

"And now here we are." His smile was slow and easy. "Tell me the best way to get this off. I'm feeling impatient, and I don't want to rip it."

She'd always dreamed of having a forthright lover instead of the tentative boys she'd stumbled into bed with in the past. In truth, she'd given that imaginary lover Sam's face. Now fantasy and reality had combined. And she already knew her lines.

"Better yet, let me show you the best way to get it off." Moving a step back, she leaned down, clutched the hem in both hands and lifted the dress over her head. "How's that?"

Sam's quick intake of breath told her that she'd made the right impression standing there in only her black panties and her red shoes. She'd seen centerfolds in outfits like this, and she'd posed in front of a mirror to gauge the effect, but this was the first time she'd tried out the ensemble on a real live man.

As her dress slipped from her fingers to the floor, his gaze roamed her bare breasts and her erect nipples. She let him look. Putting herself on display excited her as much as it obviously excited him. She'd never exploited the power of her naked body before. It was more fun than she'd imagined it would be.

He gulped. "Kasey, you're...so gorgeous. I can't even find the words. You're—"

"Still not naked." She was ready for the next level of thrill seeking. She kicked off her shoes with a flourish and shimmied out of her panties.

He groaned and started ripping off his own clothes. A button popped, but he paid no attention. His focus remained fixed on Kasey as he tossed his shirt on the floor.

And there was that sexy tattoo, rippling as he hurriedly shucked his pants. At the age of eight she'd been mesmerized by that tattoo, the first one she'd ever seen up close and personal. Now the man with the tattoo was going to get very up close and personal with *her*.

She could hardly wait to get her hands on his beautiful body, but she didn't want to appear too eager. He didn't have to know that he was the best specimen she'd ever seen naked, not counting the guys in *Playgirl*. She hoped he wasn't quite as hugely endowed as some of the men in that magazine. A few of the centerfolds had dimensions that were scary for the average girl.

Anticipation had her gulping for air, so she covered that by walking to the bed and stretching out on the cool sheets. That put her at eye level with his package, which was currently straining to escape from its cotton prison. Judging from the bulge, Sam was plenty big, but any minute she'd know whether he carried around a large or a supersize model.

Then he peeled off his bikini briefs, and she was thrilled to discover he possessed wonderful proportions, proportions that could certainly satisfy but not intimidate. From this vantage point, Sam's manly attributes were truly inspiring, and her complementary parts had indeed become very inspired, responding with a rush of moisture.

Sam pulled out the bedside-table drawer, took out a box and set it down next to the lamp. "Now." He crawled in beside her. "Come here."

7

THE MOMENT WHEN Sam gathered Kasey's warm, supple body close and kissed her smiling mouth felt so incredibly right it made his head spin. He'd never believed in love at first sight, but this woman had slipped into his life, into his bed, like the missing piece of a puzzle. She had the perfect touch, the perfect scent, the perfect voice.

She belonged in this house, in this bed, in his arms. And he would show her exactly how much. Kissing her with all the certainty he felt, he rolled her to her back. She spread her thighs, and he could have taken advantage, burying himself inside her without stopping to put on a condom. He wondered if one day he'd be able to do that because caution wouldn't be important.

Maybe. But first many things had to happen. And at the head of the line was a night of pure pleasure. Although he wanted nothing more than to enter her and make that ultimate connection, he knew that most women expected to be led gradually to that point. And he was only too happy to guide her.

Sam intended to leave no sensual stone unturned tonight. Whatever she needed to make this an unforgettable experience, he'd provide. He lifted his lips from hers. "Tell me what you like. Tell me how I can make you happy."

Her breath came in quick little puffs, breaking up her words. "I'll bet...you already...know."

He nibbled her earlobe. "Generally, I might. I want specifics."

She moaned softly and wiggled beneath him. "And I want...something very specific."

"Then tell me."

Panting, she reached between their hot bodies and curled her fingers around his penis. "This."

His heart thundered in his ears. The pressure of her fingers was nearly enough to set him off. "Now?"

"Right now, Sam." She fondled him, creating havoc with his control.

He drew away, afraid he'd lose it. "But I was going to... What about foreplay?"

"We've had...hours of...foreplay. Do me."

He believed her. Only a fool would keep questioning when a woman spoke that plainly. "You've got it." He rolled to his side and made rapid work of opening a condom packet. By the time he returned to her, she was looking at him with undisguised longing.

Blood pounded through his veins as he moved between her thighs and braced himself on his knees and hands. "I thought it was only guys who liked to go straight to the main event."

She grasped his hips. "Wrong."

"I'm glad to be wrong." Watching her eyes, he probed gently, found that sweet door to nirvana and shoved home. There, that was what he wanted to see in her expression, the same sense of wonder he was feeling. He'd had plenty of sex in his life, but this was different, more significant somehow.

She felt wonderfully snug, as if the two of them had been created to make this connection with no room to spare. Somehow he'd known they'd fit like this. Maybe she had, too, and that's why she'd insisted they forget the preliminaries.

"Better, now?" he asked softly.

Her rapid breathing made her breasts quiver. "Much better."

"I still want to kiss you all over. You have such kiss-able breasts. I want to run my tongue over each nipple, and then—why are you smiling?"

"Thinking how nice that will be...later. But I can't wait for you to do all that."

He drew back and pushed in again. "Even if I kissed you until I made you come?"

That idea registered in her eyes. "I would like that."

"I think you would."

"But right now, I need you here inside me."

"Then I can guess what else you need." He began a slow rhythm. With the perfect fit they had, he suspected she'd feel every thrust in all the right places.

She moaned softly. "Good guess."

"Remember, no common walls." He picked up the pace. "You can be as loud as you want." He'd never tested that. This would be the first time in his house. He was glad she was here to test it with him.

"Mmm." She closed her eyes and lifted her hips slightly. "Ooh. Mmm, yeah. Right there."

He took his cue and snagged a pillow. "Lift up a little more."

She opened her eyes. "But it's...it's good like this."

"I know. But you'll get tired holding yourself up.

Lift." When she did, he tucked the pillow under her. "Tell me how that feels." He slid slowly in and out, stroking steadily.

Her eyes became unfocused and her lips parted. "Like...heaven. Like we're doing it on a cloud. Oh, that's very *good*."

He felt ridiculously happy that he'd found a way to share some of his expertise with her and increase her pleasure. The angle did a few special things for him, too, so he'd have to exercise some control. Gliding back and forth like this was building the tension to a dangerous level.

When he felt her start to tighten around him, alerting him that she was on the brink, he bit down on his bottom lip to stop the surge of his own climax. She affected him so strongly that he'd have to work on his stamina when having sex with her. But what fun work it would be.

She began to whimper.

"That's it." He increased the tempo, but that made his own climax edge closer. He thought about frogs and kept going. "Come on, yell for me, Kasey. Show me what you're made of."

Her whimpers became cries, and she dug her fingers into his back.

He rode her harder, coaxing her into ever louder moans. "Let me hear you come!" he yelled, pumping faster. "Come for me!" And as if obeying his command, she came, shouting and laughing as her body bucked against his.

Only the image of frogs kept him from following right after. As she quivered beneath him, he thrust gently, absorbing the aftershocks, hoping to keep her on the edge.

She opened her eyes, a question there.

"Again," he murmured. "Show me that move again."

"I...I can't..."

"Sure you can." Easing slowly in and out, he reached down and rubbed his thumb over her happy spot.

She gasped.

"See?" He continued a circular motion with his thumb and watched her expression change from doubt to excitement.

This time she was loud from the get-go, groaning and urging him on, wrapping her legs around him, abandoning herself to the possibility of another climax. Already the dynamic had changed between them. He could feel her trusting him now to take her where she wanted to go. And he would do that.

But as he pushed her closer, he knew that he couldn't hold back this time. The erotic sensation of touching her there, right where he could feel the pressure of each thrust of his penis, was too much stimulation. When she went off like a rocket, so did he, bellowing out his sexual satisfaction, loving the sense of privacy that allowed him to do it.

Sex in a house was good. Sex in a house with Kasey was *very* good.

NOT LONG AFTER THAT, Kasey took a tour of the house while wearing Sam's shirt and nothing else. She wasn't sure that a tour of the house was a wise idea, considering that she would end all contact with Sam after tonight, but he'd been like a little kid with a new toy. He'd admitted that he'd only had the house six months and she was his first female guest.

That had worried her, too. Sam might be putting too much importance on what was happening between them, even though she'd given him no reason to do that. She knew from talking with her friends that lots of couples enjoyed a night of sex with no strings attached. Sam was thirty, for heaven's sake. He had to know that was a possibility.

But you haven't said that, whispered a little voice in her head. She should have. She should have said it on the dance floor, or in the car, or before they walked into his house, or before he took off his clothes. But she'd never tried out that particular line, and it didn't come trippingly off the tongue, as Shakespeare would say.

She would tell him though, and soon, because this affair couldn't go anywhere. He was a thirty-year-old guy with a *house,* for heaven's sake. She was a twenty-year-old with no desire to settle down. They were very different.

She had to keep that thought front and center in her mind, especially considering how good the sex had been. She'd never had a multi before. Add that to the privacy of being alone in a house, another luxury she'd never experienced, and the comfy bed, and his trick with the pillow—way too much fun.

Then there was the other problem, the sense of belonging. She'd started this date already slightly in love with Sam, and he'd more than lived up to her expectations. They got along very well, considering how old he was. More than once she'd caught herself wondering if she could stretch this episode beyond one night. But she knew that would be a mistake that could get her in serious trouble.

Putting her thoughts temporarily on hold, she went for a tour of the house, because he seemed to need her to see it. Maybe that's the way new home owners were about their houses—they felt the need to show them off to anyone who would look around. She wouldn't know about that, but she had to admit it was a very nice house.

"I still have plenty I want to do to the place." Dressed in a pair of shorts he'd grabbed from a drawer, Sam held her hand as he took her back through the living room. "But at least the previous owners had already pulled up all the carpet and refinished the wood floors."

"They feel nice." She'd never walked on real wooden floors in her bare feet, and she liked the sensation.

He glanced down at her feet. "I know what you mean. I hardly ever wear shoes in here." His eyes traveled upward, to where the shirt skimmed her thighs. "Too bad I took down the drapes, or we wouldn't have to wear clothes, either." His eyes grew hot and his fingers tightened.

The thought of walking around Sam's house naked spiked her arouse-o-meter. "I'd probably feel weird doing that," she said. But she didn't really think so. She suspected she'd feel sexy.

"You'd get used to it. I never realized I was so sick of roommates and apartment living until I moved here. Come on, let me show you the best part."

She'd seen the best part, and it was his king-size bed, but she chose not to say so. The more she praised his lovemaking techniques, the less he'd understand when she told him goodbye.

He drew her through the dining room, which currently had only his computer desk in it, and into the kitchen, where he flipped on another light. "This is not the best part. Eventually the kitchen will have to be completely renovated, but I'm waiting. Kitchens aren't my specialty."

She could guess what he was waiting for—a woman who wanted to share this house with him, a woman who would have definite ideas about how she liked her kitchen arranged. "It looks okay to me," she said, so that he'd understand she wasn't mentally redesigning the space to suit her. She didn't even like to cook.

He shrugged. "It works for now. Which reminds me, would you like something? I have some wine and beer, plus I think there's cheese and crackers, if you're hungry."

"No, no, I'm fine." She turned down the goodies quickly, alarmed by her urge to accept them and watch him putter around this ancient kitchen. She was becoming entirely too involved with him. Time to get back to the sex.

"Okay, then let me show you the back." He unlocked the kitchen door and opened it. "Someday I'll have this widened and put in French doors, probably during the kitchen renovation. I'll also have somebody replace the bedroom window with French doors so it opens out here, too." Still holding her hand, he started through the door.

"Wait, are we going out there?"

He paused. "Why not?"

"I'm wearing nothing but your shirt, and there's a button missing."

"Doesn't matter. There's a flagstone patio and the yard is surrounded by a seven-foot solid wall. It's like a secret garden. No one can see in. This backyard was the main reason I bought the house."

"So you could have parties?" Somehow she didn't think so.

"I suppose, but more for myself. A hideaway." He gave her hand a tug. "It's okay. Trust me, nothing will get you."

She'd been an Arizona girl too long to walk casually outside barefoot. "What about scorpions? What about snakes?"

"No snakes in this garden. The wall's too high. And I patrol all the time with a black light and I've never seen a single scorpion. I think we're too far away from the actual desert here in the middle of town." He smiled at her. "But if it would make you feel better, I'll find you something to wear on your feet."

"No, I'll take your word for it." She almost wished he'd made fun of her fears instead of being so understanding. It was going to make dumping him extremely difficult. Of course, once she dumped him, he wouldn't be understanding. He'd pretty much hate her. What a depressing thought.

The cool night air tickled her bare legs as she stepped outside onto the flagstone. Low pagoda lights ringed the patio, which was furnished with a glass table and chairs on one side and a rope hammock hanging from a metal frame on the other. She smelled flowers and heard water splashing softly. Despite the seven-foot wall, which she could see dimly in the glow from the half moon, she felt daring being out here wearing only Sam's shirt.

"Isn't this fantastic?" Sam swung his arm to encompass the area. "Those two mesquite trees shade the patio during the day, and once I gave them a good trim they look really good."

Kasey glanced up through the delicate herringbone pattern of the mesquite leaves to the night sky, where the moon was the main attraction. City lights blocked out most of the stars. Although she could hear the muted drone of traffic, the trickling water and chirping crickets turned the yard into an oasis of calm in the middle of the city.

She could picture herself in the hammock reading a good book. She could also picture herself in the hammock with Sam, but she blocked that image. A hammock was for spending a lazy Sunday afternoon together, but impractical for sex. All she wanted from Sam was satisfaction, not long-term friendship.

"I can see why you like it," she said.

"I put in the pond and waterfall myself." He sounded very proud of that.

"I can hear it. Where is it?"

"Over here." He led her to the side of the yard, near the hammock. "I nestled it in between the lantana and the hibiscus, and tried to make it look as natural as possible."

Leaning closer, Kasey could see little silver flashes as moonlight reflected off water tumbling down levels of smooth rock into a small pool. "What a great idea. Do you have fish?"

"Not yet, but I've been thinking about it." He rubbed her palm with his thumb as he stood beside her, staring at the waterfall.

"Fish would be cool." In spite of her vow not to get drawn into his life, she'd been captured by his excitement when he talked of this backyard.

"See, this is how I want to expand Ashton Landscaping. I'm known for creating and maintaining commercial installations, but I want to reach the individual home owner who would like something like this, a retreat. I think we're moving away from flashy showplace yards and toward increased privacy. I want that kind of business."

Now was the time to squash his next move. Then she could give her speech about spur-of-the-moment sex that meant nothing and went nowhere. "Sam, about hiring me, I don't think—"

"But I do think." He pulled her gently into his arms. "I never trusted the idea of bringing in a PR expert until I met you, but I know you'd do a great job. This new direction would take more than buying some ads. I need a new image." He slipped his hands under the hem of her shirt and cupped her bottom.

"That could be, but I can't be the one to give it to you." She wanted to give him something else, though. The moment he'd started caressing her, she'd remembered his promise to kiss her until she climaxed. From the way she felt right now, that wouldn't take very many kisses.

"Why not?" He started unfastening the buttons of her shirt.

"Because of this...what we're doing..." She closed her eyes and sighed as he pushed aside the shirt and stroked her breast.

"That's silly." He leaned down and nuzzled the side of her neck. "What happens here is a private thing," he murmured. "It doesn't have to affect our business relationship, except to make it better."

She felt confused, not to mention aroused. She'd thought there was some sort of rule about not sleeping with your clients. If there wasn't, there should be. Shouldn't there? "I don't think it's right. I don't—" She paused, unable to remember what she'd meant to say because he'd leaned down to flick his tongue over her nipple.

"Mmm." He licked her other breast. "You taste delicious."

A cool breeze made her damp nipples tingle. Vaguely she realized the shirt now hung open all the way to her thighs. "Maybe...maybe we should go in."

"Are you cold?"

Not even remotely. Now he'd started to suck on her nipples, and she was getting hotter by the minute. "I just thought, that if we're going to...get down to it...then we should go back to your bedroom." He was turning her knees to jelly again, and before much longer she wouldn't be able to walk.

He kissed his way back to her mouth. "Or we could stay here," he murmured.

"But—"

"Let's try this. Sit down here." He guided her to the edge of the hammock.

She was so wobbly that she sat down immediately. "Oh!"

"What?" He knelt in front of her.

"That feels very funky on my tush." Weird and on the kinky side, too, she thought.

He steadied her by bracketing her hips. "Bad funky or interesting funky?"

"Interesting." She was curious as to what he had in mind. She couldn't imagine having sex with him on this thing.

"Then let's go with it." He cupped her face and feathered kisses over her mouth. "I want you to lie straight back."

"And what will you do?"

"Stay right here."

She was beginning to get the picture, and it was quite a picture. He wanted her crossways on the hammock, her legs dangling over the edge, while he moved in. Her pulse rate accelerated. "You're sure no one can see us?"

"Positive." His voice trembled with obvious excitement.

"Not even the eye-in-the-sky police helicopter?"

"If I hear it coming, I'll throw myself across your writhing body."

She started to quiver. "And will I be writhing?"

"That's my goal." He nibbled on her bottom lip. "Only thing is, you can't yell out here."

She really needed to tell him that tonight was all

they'd enjoy together, and she would, but not now, not before the hammock experiment. "Okay. I'll be quiet."

"Good. Now lie back." He leaned over her as he guided her down. As he did, he moved his mouth to her breasts, then on to her tummy. When her head rested on the far side of the hammock, he kissed the moist curls between her legs. "Perfect."

She couldn't believe she was doing this, lying in a rope hammock looking up at the moon, her shirt open, her heart racing because any moment Sam would...and then he did, using his warm tongue in a way that made her gasp. She pushed her fingers through the gaps in the hammock's weave and hung on for dear life. Oh, he was good. He was *very* good.

Then, when she thought the sensations rolling over her couldn't get any better, he thrust two fingers up through the open weave and buried them deep inside her. Incredible. As he used his tongue to swirl and lap, he stroked rapidly with his fingers until she was on complete overload. Her orgasm roared in with such force that she had to clench her jaw to muffle her groans of completion.

"Sweet," he murmured, trailing kisses along her thighs.

She lay panting, boneless and unable to move. Slowly her fingers uncurled from their death grip on the hammock. He'd have to carry her inside. No way could she walk there. Maybe he really did plan to carry her, because he lifted her hips to scoot her a little closer to the edge.

She took a shaky breath. "I can try to walk," she said.

"Not yet. Stay right there."

No problem. She would stay right there and look up at that beautiful, beautiful moon. Sex was the best thing ever, especially delivered by Sam.

"I'm going to hook your ankles over my shoulders."

"You're going to do what?" She raised her head as best she could and discovered that he was kneeling across from her, her ankles propped on his shoulders. He'd moved very close to the hammock. Then, she felt the smooth glide of his penis entering her. "Sam?"

"Hold still." His voice was husky.

"Did you put on a—"

"Yes. Put one in my pocket before we came out here."

"You had this in mind all along!"

"Not exactly this." His chuckle was low and sexy. "This was a recent inspiration. Now, I'm going to gently swing the hammock. It might not work, but if it does..."

"You're insane."

"Want to go insane with me?"

She should have picked someone else for her first one-night stand. Sam was more than she could handle. She felt his charisma wrap around her like the ropes of the hammock. With a guy like Sam, you always wanted to find out what would happen next.

"Sure," she said.

8

SAM WONDERED if knowing about Kasey's super brain had spurred him to become more creative. Or maybe it was the house and this special garden he loved so much. They'd already done the wild thing on an ordinary bed. He thought they should try other options now.

And the hammock was some option. He didn't have to swing it very fast to get excellent friction. He'd read about something similar to this, some Asian rope trick, but the hammock worked just fine. More than fine.

Kasey was making soft little moaning sounds that he thought meant she was having a good time, too. But maybe he'd better check.

"You okay?" he murmured as he eased the hammock back and forth.

"Oh, yeah." She gulped for air. "This is...amazing. I don't have to...do anything and still I'm getting...my jollies."

"Then it's working for you?" It was working so well for him that he calculated about thirty seconds to blast-off.

"It's working. It's really, really working."

"Good." He tightened his grip on the edge of the hammock. The creaking of the metal support rings merged with the chirp of crickets. The flagstone was tough on his knees, but the rest of him was so happy he didn't care about his knees. "I'm...I'm close."

She groaned. "Me, too."

"Really close."

"Yeah. Like...right...*now*. Oh. Oh, oh, *oh*."

As her spasms rippled over his rigid penis, he steadied the hammock and let his own orgasm take over, clenching his jaw against the cries that rose from his throat. He'd meant to be quieter, but the pleasure was too intense to take it in silence. He hoped the neighbors were in bed asleep, because if they happened to be outside, they'd know exactly what was going on.

And maybe that didn't matter. At the moment, he really didn't care what the neighbors thought. He didn't care about a damned thing, actually, except enjoying this wonderful night with Kasey.

KASEY ALLOWED SAM to untangle them from their complicated position so she could stretch out lengthwise on the hammock. She murmured her thanks, feeling sexy and very sophisticated. Not every woman could say she'd had this experience. Kasey didn't intend to tell anyone about it, though, not even if it would give her hoochie mama status in the office.

Next to her, the waterfall babbled away, letting her imagine they were out in the woods next to a mountain stream. She didn't feel like moving, or thinking. "Let's stay here a little while," she said. Then she shivered as a breeze cooled her skin.

"We'll stay, but we need a blanket." Sam dropped a kiss on her mouth and headed into the house.

A blanket would be cozy, Kasey realized. Maybe too

cozy. As the glow from her recent orgasm faded, she began to wonder when she should ask Sam to take her home. She really didn't want to do that, but she'd have to force herself at some point.

When he dropped her off at her apartment would be the time to tell him she wouldn't be seeing him anymore. Bringing up the subject in advance wasn't smart. She might not have the willpower to make it stick. But at her front door, she could say what had to be said and then go inside, which would be easier on both of them.

She should probably think about leaving soon. The longer she stayed, the worse the parting would be. But now she'd agreed to this snuggle-under-a-blanket routine, and he'd gone to the trouble of finding a blanket.

It must be some trouble, because he wasn't coming right back. Finally he showed up, a plastic water bottle in one hand, a box of crackers in the other and a blanket under his arm.

"I thought we needed eats," he said.

"Nice idea." So he'd been getting refreshments. He was too sweet for his own good, plus she thought it was cute that he'd brought a bottle of water when that had been what she'd offered him earlier in the day. She really hated to think of dumping him when the night was over. She wondered if there was any way to avoid doing that. She quickly analyzed the situation. No, she had to dump him.

He set the water bottle and the crackers on the flagstone. "A man—not to mention a woman—does not live by sex alone." He grinned at her as he unfolded the blanket and draped it over the hammock. "But it sure would be fun trying."

"Uh-huh." Other than movie-star crushes, there'd never been a guy she'd choose over a plate of excellent pasta. Sam had demonstrated that sex with him was better than anything else on the menu.

Once the blanket was arranged, he attempted to crawl into the hammock beside Kasey and nearly toppled her onto the ground.

"Hey!" She started laughing as she hung on to the wildly swinging hammock. "I thought you knew your way around these things!"

"Are you kidding?" He climbed out again and grabbed the edge to slow it down. "I just bought it last week. This is its maiden voyage."

"Really?" She wished he hadn't told her that. When she cut him loose, the hammock might be ruined for him, and here it was, brand-new.

"I bought it with the idea that I'd lie out here and read, but so far I haven't taken the time." He started to get in again. "This can't be that tough."

"Hold on. I have a suggestion." Kasey didn't know much about hammocks, either, but she was good at problem-solving. "I'll put one foot on the ground. When you climb in, leave one foot on the ground. Then we'll keep it balanced and lift both feet off at the same time."

"Makes sense." He waited for her to position her foot on the flagstone. Then he carefully eased in beside her, leaving one of his feet planted firmly on the other side.

"That's it. Now, on three—one, two, *three*." The hammock swayed slightly, but they were both in, snug as two bugs under the blanket.

"That's what I love about smart women," he said. "They're full of good ideas."

"Thanks." Not every guy thought she was full of good ideas. She'd met a few who insisted on doing things their way, even if their way wasn't working. Sam didn't seem to let his ego run the show. He'd make a good catch for some lucky woman.

"Now for the goodies." He reached down and picked up the water bottle. "Have a swig."

"Don't mind if I do." She popped the nozzle and took a drink. It wasn't water. "Wine?"

"Yeah. The connoisseurs would have a fit if they caught me serving Chardonnay in a water bottle, but it's easier to drink this way here, and besides, the bottle's sort of symbolic of how we met."

Don't do that. She didn't want him getting sentimental. That would make the inevitable that much tougher. "It sure is a great delivery system if you're lying in a hammock."

"That's what I thought." He opened the cracker box and held it toward her. "I hope you like wheat crackers."

"Love 'em." She took one and popped it into her mouth. "Have some wine." She passed the bottle over.

"We could pretend this is one of those goatskin flasks they used to have in the olden days." He poured a stream of wine into his open mouth.

She watched him and smiled. "This is fun."

He swallowed the wine and turned to look into her eyes. "It is fun. Thanks for christening the hammock with me. That was incredible."

"Sure was." She still got quivers of sensation thinking about it. "Do you think anybody heard us?"

"If they did, at least they didn't call the police. But it's late. I'm sure everyone else is asleep."

"You should probably be asleep, too. Tomorrow's a workday."

He chewed and swallowed a cracker. "Ask me if I care."

"Do you care?" she asked, laughing.

"No. Do you?"

"No."

"Good. Have some more wine."

She drank it the way he had, directing a stream from the pop-up top into her open mouth.

"I'm getting the urge to kiss you again."

Swallowing the wine, she glanced over at him. He'd turned on his side and was looking at her the way she imagined a fox surveyed the henhouse. But if he acted on the impulse she saw lurking in his eyes, he'd send them both sprawling to the flagstone. "There is no way in hell we can get wild when we're both on this hammock," she said.

"I know. I've already tried to imagine whether it would be possible, and I think one of us would wreck something valuable in the process." He reached behind him to deposit the box of crackers on the patio. Then he slipped his hand under the blanket and explored until he found her breast. "I just want to make out a little," he said, caressing her gently. "Nothing heavy."

She loved being petted like that, and now that he'd planted the idea, she found herself wanting to feel his lips on hers again, too. "Okay." She set the water bottle on the other side of the hammock and turned to him.

"Okay." He cupped her cheek and edged closer. The hammock swayed but didn't threaten to dump them. "Hold still, now."

"I've heard that line before."

"You were wonderful to humor me about that." He touched his mouth to hers, then ran his tongue along her lower lip.

"I was curious to see if you could manage it."

"*We* managed it." Then he settled in and started seriously kissing her.

Nice, she thought as he applied exactly the right amount of pressure, all the while massaging her breasts and teasing her nipples. After that, she forgot to evaluate. Sam's brand of kissing bypassed her brain and headed straight for her nerve endings, making them sizzle and pop, creating aches and needs and urges that prompted her to caress him in return.

She knew full well where his central operation was located. When she rubbed her hand over the fly of his shorts, she discovered his claim that he only wanted to make out a little had not been truth-in-advertising. He was ready to rumble.

He lifted his mouth a fraction away from hers. "What are you doing?"

"Testing. I thought this was going to be low-pressure sex."

"I admit I can't kiss you without getting hard. So sue me."

She smiled. "Want to go inside?"

"Nope. I really like it out here. We'll take a break and drink wine. We'll have a conversation."

Conversations made her nervous. She unfastened his shorts. "I have a better idea."

"Kasey, we'll dump."

"If you lie still, we won't." Unzipping his fly, she gradually scooted toward the foot of the hammock. It trembled but didn't tip.

"Something tells me I'd be a wise man to follow orders."

"I think you would." She was no expert at this, but from her brief experience, she didn't think men required perfection. Hampered by the unsteady nature of the hammock, she couldn't move much, either. But she could take his penis into her mouth.

Apparently that pleased him, because he groaned in ecstasy.

Being careful not to rock the hammock, she did the best she could with her tongue. From the way he was breathing like a freight train, she must be accomplishing something worthwhile. Using gentle suction and a swirling motion with her tongue, she soon had him trembling so violently she decided to finish him off before they ended up in a heap on the flagstone, after all.

Applying greater suction, she moved her head up and down just enough to provide some friction. That was all it took. His breath hissed out between his clenched teeth as he erupted.

He was still gasping for air when she inched her way back up and nestled in beside him. A man became so vulnerable at a time like this, she thought. She'd intended the move to delay conversation between them.

Conversation could only lead to trouble, but as it turned out, she was in trouble, anyway. She was becoming very softhearted about Sam Ashton.

THEY WEREN'T GETTING much talking done, Sam had to admit. But he didn't know a guy in the world who would complain about that considering the way they'd occupied their time. He couldn't have guessed that Kasey would be willing to do what she'd just done so that he wouldn't be in sexual distress. What a woman.

"Wine?" she asked once his breathing had returned to normal.

"You're fantastic." He slipped his arm around her and kissed her talented mouth. "Thank you."

"I was a little hampered by conditions."

"I couldn't tell." He took the water bottle and drank a couple of swallows of wine, congratulating himself for thinking of a way they could have it out here without spilling it all over themselves. Maybe Kasey's intelligence was rubbing off.

As she settled into the crook of his arm, he passed the wine back to her. "Crackers?"

"Sure."

Wedging the box between them, he waited for her to take some before getting a handful for himself. "I think what I like about this garden is how simple everything seems when I'm out here."

"That's an illusion, you know." She munched on some crackers.

"Maybe, maybe not. Take the way we met. We saw each other today, made a date, and here we are. Everything just worked out."

"I guess that's true." She handed him the wine.

He took another drink, savoring the smooth taste that was only slightly tainted with plastic. All the exercise, good sex and now the wine was taking its toll. He was getting sleepy. He blinked to stay awake. Sooner or later he'd have to take Kasey home. They both had to work in the morning, and she didn't have a change of clothes here.

Someday that situation could be different. Ordinarily he wouldn't be planning a long-term relationship after one night, but this date had been far from ordinary. Certainly Kasey would agree with him on that.

"Would you rather sleep a little here?" he murmured, hoping she'd say yes. "I'm sure the birds will wake us up in plenty of time."

No answer.

"Kasey?" He turned his head to check on her.

She lay with her cheek pillowed against his outstretched arm, fast asleep.

Carefully he closed the cracker box and set it on the flagstone along with the water bottle. Then he settled back with a sigh and gazed up at the half moon. In a few days the moon would be full. He'd like to be right here on that night, snuggling with Kasey. With the way things had gone so far, he saw no reason that wouldn't happen.

A GARBAGE TRUCK in the alley behind the wall woke Sam from a most excellent dream in which he seemed to be getting married. In the dream, he'd been very excited about the idea. Then his night with Kasey came flooding back, and he knew how his mind had made that leap to a wedding.

But he had more immediate concerns, like getting her back home so she wouldn't be late for work. The garbage truck came about seven-thirty, so they had no time to waste. Still, he didn't want to startle her. They could both end up sprawled on the cold hard patio if she moved too abruptly.

He'd lost all feeling in the arm she'd used to support her head, so he reached over with his other arm and held her steady while he murmured her name.

"What?" She came instantly awake and tried to struggle upright.

"Easy, babe. Easy." Fortunately he had the presence of mind to slam one foot on the ground to anchor them, or they would have tipped. Her trick. He really did like knowing she was so smart.

She groaned and flopped back onto his numb arm. "What time is it?"

"About seven-thirty."

"Yikes! We have to get going! Omigosh. Help me out of here, Sam!"

He smiled to himself. "One foot out, just like we got in." Obviously he'd have to be the calm one in a crisis. That was okay. He liked that role.

"Oh. Right. Okay, I have one foot out. Do you have one foot out?"

"I do. Good morning, by the way."

"We don't have time for good mornings. Ready? On three. One, two, *three*."

He scrambled out of the hammock and stood shaking his tingling arm. "All right. Now we'll—"

"I'll be dressed in two minutes." She ran across the patio barefoot and threw open his kitchen door.

He shook his head. She was more panicked than he'd expected. Sure, being late for work wasn't a great idea, but it wasn't a total disaster. Ten years ago he might have thought that, but he'd learned that the world didn't revolve around him. Maybe she'd made a habit of being late in the past and had no leeway with her boss.

In that case, he'd do all he could to get her home in time. After picking up the water bottle and crackers, he walked into the house in search of his wallet and keys.

He didn't have to search far. She was already headed down the hall holding his shoes in one hand and his wallet and keys in the other. His dad had a saying for this—being given the bum's rush.

"I guess being late for work is a really bad thing," he said.

"I don't want my boss to think I'm irresponsible." She handed him his shoes.

Fortunately they were loafers, and he could slip right into them. He took the wallet and keys and decided he'd drive her there without worrying about a shirt. "Being late once would brand you as irresponsible?"

"Maybe not." She looked harried and young, especially now that most of her makeup was gone. "But I don't want to take that chance."

"I'm sorry I put you in this position, then." He unlocked the front door and ushered her out. "I'll get you home as fast as possible."

"Thank you."

He decided against conversation on the way to her

place. Then she'd know he was putting all his concentration on his driving. He got her there in record time and was proud of himself. If she took a short shower and skipped breakfast, she'd make it to work on time.

She hopped out the minute he stopped the car. "Thanks, Sam."

"Can I see you tonight?"

She hesitated, uneasiness in her expression. "Well, the thing is, I—"

"Oh, yeah. You had something going on tonight. I remember now. So I'll call you later today. We'll work it out."

"Okay. See you." She hurried up the walkway to her apartment complex.

He watched her go and cursed himself for not waking up earlier. This wasn't how their fantastic night was supposed to end, with her feeling so rushed that they couldn't even say a proper goodbye or make another date. He wished she'd at least smiled and said she'd had a great time. Apparently her worry about being late wasn't allowing her to do that.

With a sigh, he put his car in Reverse and then drove home.

9

"DAMN, DAMN, DAMN," Kasey muttered as she whipped through her shower and threw on clean clothes. She hadn't been able to deliver the final blow, after all. How could she, when there was no time to spare, no time to break it to him gently?

Only a mean person would have been able to chop Sam off at the knees when there was zero time to give a compassionate goodbye speech. She hadn't planned on a long one, but at least long enough to explain that it wasn't his fault. So she'd reluctantly postponed saying what needed to be said.

Maybe she shouldn't be so paranoid about being late, but Mr. Beckworth had voiced reservations about hiring someone so young, claiming that a woman her age might not take the job seriously enough. It was a dumb prejudice on his part, but she'd proceeded to bend over backward to prove how responsible she was. Besides, there was a staff meeting this morning, and her lateness would be noticed for sure.

Because she couldn't explain all that to Sam without revealing her age, she'd had to let him think she was a nut case about punctuality. She did like to be on time, and at Beckworth, she'd made certain she was *always* on time. Mr. Beckworth had commented favorably on that more than once.

But what bothered her more than anything at the moment was that in the cold light of day, she realized she'd completely messed up her Bad Girl routine. All she'd meant to do was make Sam drool a little and then walk away. Instead she'd slept with him after convincing herself that having sex would ruin his idea of hiring her for PR work.

In fact, she'd been looking for an excuse, any excuse, to satisfy her lust. Her reasoning had been faulty, because Sam couldn't understand why having sex meant they couldn't work together. And he was right—if she didn't tell anyone what she'd done, which of course she wouldn't. Had she only flirted and walked away, she could have bragged about that to her cohorts. But she'd turned over the goods. No glory in that.

When she pulled into the parking lot next to the office building that housed Beckworth, it seemed impossible that only one day had passed. Just yesterday morning she'd parked her car here, vaguely aware of a man in a truck behind her, a man who might have accidentally leaned on the horn. Just yesterday she'd seen Sam Ashton, the object of her childhood crush, manicuring a tree in front of the Beckworth windows. And she'd drawn the long straw.

She was glad for the meeting this morning, which would give her an hour or so to rehearse her story. And she would be on time, just barely. Sam had navigated the streets with the intensity of a NASCAR driver so that she'd make it to work okay.

The tree he'd trimmed actually did look like a piece of sculpture now, with bare lower limbs undulating upward to a canopy of feathered branches. She remembered how hard he'd worked all day before spending a long, physically demanding night with her. He must be in pretty good shape for thirty, because he'd never complained about being tired.

She'd had a much easier day, and yet she'd been the first one to fall asleep. His gentle voice and the music of the waterfall had lulled her into dreamland. What a night it had been. And what a mess she'd created.

She rode the elevator alone and slipped into the office conference room just as Arnold Beckworth opened the meeting. While Beckworth talked about aggressively pursuing new accounts, Kasey's buddies kept glancing at her, either smirking or waggling their eyebrows questioningly. They were obviously dying to pump her about her date with Tarzan of the Chain Saw.

How ironic that Beckworth would be on a tear about pursuing new business and she was trying to get rid of a potential client as quickly as possible. She'd have to wait for Sam to call her, though. Because he'd picked her up, she hadn't needed his home phone number, and during their exciting date she hadn't thought to ask for it. She hesitated to call him at work because he might be climbing trees again and answering a phone call would be difficult. Besides, she didn't want him to think she was eager to be in touch with him.

But when he called, and she knew he would, she planned to suggest another meeting tonight, but this time for something simple like coffee. If they met early, around seven, she might still be able to drop in on her mom's basket party later. She wasn't into collecting baskets or any of that domestic stuff, but her mother was, and Kasey had decided to order something for her mom's birthday. It wouldn't be a surprise, but it would help her mother's sales count and give her a gift she really wanted, all at the same time.

Sam needed a more domestic woman who cared about baskets and kitchen appliances and gardening. All Kasey cared about was sex. That might intrigue him for the time being, but eventually he'd expect her to develop more mature interests. After all, he owned a *house*. She kept coming back to that, hoping the thought of Sam Ashton, home owner, would blot out the thought of Sam Ashton, fabulous lover.

Of course the great sex wasn't all of it, either. He was just plain adorable, with his water bottle full of wine and his box of crackers. He'd been so proud of his little house, and the yard where he'd created an oasis of calm. They hadn't been particularly calm last night. They'd made that hammock creak pretty loud.

"Kasey? Kasey, are you still with us?"

Startled, she glanced up and realized Beckworth had addressed her directly. And she'd been dreaming about Sam. She cleared her throat and hoped her cheeks weren't as rosy as they felt. "Sure am, Mr. Beckworth. Just now I was brainstorming how I might pull in some additional business."

"And that was my question, Kasey." He peered at her over his reading glasses as light glanced off his polished head. His response to growing bald had been to shave the hair that was left. "All of us have contacts who could become clients—people in our congregation at church, friends we meet at our country club, even family members. So who have you come up with?"

She should have known he'd pin her to the wall. He was convinced the younger generation had no attention span, and he'd just caught her staring off into space when she was supposed to be hanging on his every word. "I'm already talking to a potential client, and he may lead me to other accounts in that field," she said.

"Excellent. Who would that be?"

Of course he'd ask. She whipped out another line of BS. "I hesitate to announce who it is until I've worked out a few more details." She had no intention of following through with Sam, but maybe she could buy some time.

Beckworth frowned. "Surely you could give us the name of the business, Kasey. We all understand that prospects can change their minds."

"Well, he asked me to keep our negotiations quiet until he'd decided for sure. It's a delicate situation." Was it ever.

"Very well." Beckworth obviously didn't like it, and he'd probably question her privately later, but he dropped the subject for now. "That means we've heard from everyone, then. I'll expect reports from each of you on your progress by the end of next week."

Sure enough, he spoke up before she could leave the conference room. "May I see you a moment, Kasey?" He stood and began gathering his papers into a leather briefcase.

"Of course." She straightened her shoulders and tried to look older.

Beckworth waited until the others had left the conference room. "In general, I've been very happy with your performance," he said. "You show remarkable ability in one so young."

"Thank you, Mr. Beckworth." She accepted his patronizing attitude because she owed him a lot. Beckworth was known throughout the Valley, and her work here would look great on her résumé if she decided to take a job outside Arizona. Her folks had begged her not to move for another couple of years, but someday she might try L.A. on for size.

Beckworth cleared his throat. "In fact, this morning is the first time I've seen you distracted. I'm not sure I buy your explanation. Is anything wrong?"

Omigod. He was showing his grandfatherly side, and she so didn't deserve it. She'd stayed out all night with a man and consequently wasn't at her best this morning. She didn't want him to be solicitous and kind.

She took the coward's way out. "I think I might be coming down with something." Like terminal stupidity.

"Then you should go home and rest." He looked as if he might even pat her shoulder, but seemed to change his mind at the last minute. "We're not running a slave galley, you know. And you do look a little flushed."

No kidding. Anyone would look flushed when faced by a disaster that was getting worse by the minute. She couldn't go home because then she might miss Sam's call, or worse, the receptionist would say where she was and he might come over.

When she had her talk with him they needed to be on neutral territory, someplace where he wouldn't be able to work his wiles on her. That expression had never made sense to her before, but it did now. Sam was loaded with wiles, and she was way too susceptible to them.

"I'll take it easy today," she promised Beckworth. "Thank you for being concerned."

"Of course I'm concerned. I'll admit I hired you against my better judgment, but you've proven yourself in the time you've been here. That's why I was so disconcerted by your behavior in the meeting today. It's not like you."

"It won't happen again." Kasey realized he'd spoken abruptly during the meeting because he'd been worried about her. "And thank you for keeping the secret about my age. I think it helps with office dynamics."

"I absolutely agree." He gave her a rare smile. "You have excellent potential in this field. Keep up the good work."

"Thank you." He'd never praised her like this. How ironic that he'd choose the moment when she felt like a complete dunce. "And speaking of work, I'd better get back to it." She smiled as brightly as possible and hurried out of the conference room.

Back in the main office she ignored the significant glances from Gretchen and Amy as she headed for her desk and switched on her computer.

Within two minutes Gretchen approached, a file folder in her hand. Kasey knew it was a prop. Gretchen couldn't stand the suspense another minute.

Tapping the file folder against the desk, she spoke in a low voice, no doubt worried about whether Beckworth might stroll through. "Please don't tell me that you spent your entire date with that hunk selling him on the idea of a PR campaign."

Kasey bit the inside of her lip to keep from laughing. "Uh, no."

"Oh, goodie. That means you had a hot time on the old town and you were thinking about that very thing when Beckworth nailed you for spacing out."

"Something like that." No sense trying to fool Gretchen.

"Oh, God. Listen, Myra says that Beckworth's taking off for a round of golf soon, which means that you can fill us in once he leaves. Deal?"

Kasey coughed. "Well, there's really not a lot to tell." And most of it she'd take to her grave.

"Not a lot to tell, my ass. I've never seen you as dreamy eyed as you were during the meeting. I'm guessing that—" Gretchen's eyes grew round at something on the other side of the room. "Hel-*lo*. If I'm not mistaken, Tarzan of the Chain Saw just walked in the office. And he's heading this way."

Heart thumping, Kasey swiveled her chair around and stared straight into Sam's eyes.

She watched as he headed over, looking fresh as a daisy in beige slacks and a white knit shirt with Ashton Landscaping embroidered on the pocket. A person would never believe that he'd been up most of the night, in more ways than one. Once again, she felt her cheeks grow hot as she remembered precisely what activities she'd enjoyed with him in his cozy backyard.

"Hi," he said, giving her a warm smile. "I decided to come by this morning so we could discuss that PR campaign. The receptionist said it would be fine if I just came over here to talk to you, but if you're too busy right now, we can set up another time."

"Hi, Sam." Kasey recognized Myra's handiwork. The receptionist had no doubt taken great pleasure in sending Sam right over without buzzing her desk first. Myra loved surprises.

"Sam, I'm Gretchen Davies." Gretchen stuck out her hand. "All of us here really admire your work."

"Thanks." Sam shook her hand. "I guess you had a bird's-eye view of the process yesterday."

"That we did. Very inspiring."

Kasey watched Gretchen bat her eyes at Sam and had an inspiration of her own. "About that project, Sam, I think Gretchen's the person to deal with you instead of me. She's had much more experience than I have, and I'm sure she'd have some great ideas for your new direction."

"But you already have a grasp of my concept," Sam said. "No reflection on Ms. Davies, but you're the one I want to handle everything."

"And you should handle everything, Kasey." Gretchen, the rat, actually winked at her. "I wouldn't dream of taking your hard-earned business, not when Mr. Beckworth asked us just this morning to bring in new clients. Obviously this is the lead you mentioned during the meeting, and he's all yours."

"You mentioned me during the meeting?" Sam looked pleased.

"I didn't mention you by name." Kasey hoped this was a nightmare and she'd wake up very soon.

"You could have," he said. "I was absolutely serious about hiring you. I want to do that, and if you're being asked to bring in new clients, so much the better. Here I am."

"I'll leave you two to discuss the next step," Gretchen said. "Nice meeting you, Sam."

"Same here, Gretchen." Then he turned back to Kasey. "I really can come back later if now isn't a good time. You look a little harried."

A *little* harried? She felt as if someone had tossed her insides into a blender. "Uh, no, this is fine. Please sit down."

"Okay." Sam settled into the upholstered armchair next to her desk. Then he lowered his voice. "I really do plan to hire you, but mostly I wanted to see you again. Turns out the job we had scheduled for today canceled this morning, so I had some time on my hands. I wanted to apologize for making you rush out of my house this morning. We had no chance to talk."

She didn't want to discuss that now. "It wasn't your fault."

"It was my fault. I was the host, which meant I should have made sure we woke up in plenty of time."

In spite of his low tone, Kasey worried that Sam's voice might carry to the neighboring desks. If any of her co-workers caught the phrase *made sure we woke up*, she'd never hear the end of it. She needed to put an end to speculation. "I understand that you want to *wake up* your company image," she said very clearly. "What sort of a budget are you looking at for your campaign?"

He gave her a slow smile. "Whatever it takes."

Her heart, not exactly steady in the first place, skipped a few more beats. She had to face the fact she was being wooed. She'd have to put a stop to it, of course, but it might not be easy. She eyed him nervously. In fact, the determination in his expression made it clear it would be damned tough.

As if to drive the final nail in her coffin, Beckworth approached her desk. "Kasey, if I may interrupt for a moment?"

"Certainly, Mr. Beckworth." She could guess what this was about. He wanted to be introduced to the man at her desk because he'd guessed this might be the mystery client she'd referred to, and he didn't like being kept in the dark.

Beckworth confirmed that by pausing to glance pointedly at Sam.

She had no choice but to make the introduction. "Uh, Sam Ashton, I'd like you to meet Arnold Beckworth, the head of our firm."

Sam stood and shook the older man's hand. "Glad to meet you."

Beckworth glanced at Sam's shirt pocket. "Pleased to meet you, as well. Ashton Landscaping, eh? Interested in having some PR work done, by any chance?"

"Actually, yes. Ms. Braddock and I were just discussing some of the details. She's extremely creative. I probably don't have to tell you that."

Beckworth smiled, obviously happy to have his curiosity satisfied and a new client on board so quickly. "Extremely creative," he said. "You couldn't be in more capable hands."

"I couldn't have said it better."

Kasey wanted to crawl under the desk. If Sam hadn't been thinking about sex before, he definitely was now after Beckworth's remark about capable hands. "I appreciate the confidence you both have in me," she said. Man, did that sound stuffy. Then she remembered that Beckworth still hadn't stated his alleged reason for coming over to her desk. She looked at him. "Was there something you needed to talk to me about?"

"You know, it can wait. Sorry to have interrupted you. I have a ten-thirty tee time. I'll catch you tomorrow." He held out his hand to Sam. "I'm happy you've chosen Beckworth. I know you'll be pleased with our service."

Sam returned his handshake. "Thanks. I already am. Very pleased."

Kasey gulped. That's what she got for thinking she could play with the big boys. She was in so much trouble, it wasn't even funny.

10

"WERE YOU ON TIME this morning?" Sam asked. Kasey sure was acting strange, considering how sexy and open she'd been on their date.

"I was, just barely." She turned away from him and typed in something on her computer. Then she swiveled back to face him and tucked her hair behind her ears. "Would you prefer to pay by the hour or put me on a retainer?"

"What's the difference?" He tried to keep his mind on the business at hand, instead of the way her blue silk blouse clung to her breasts and how her blond hair rippled when she moved her head.

"If we go hourly, I'll bill you every time we talk about the project. If you put me on a monthly retainer, you'll have unlimited consultation time. If you think we can wrap this up in five to ten hours, then hourly would be the way to go. If you expect it to take more than, say, fifteen hours, then you'd be money ahead to pay the retainer."

"Then I want the retainer." Unlimited time with Kasey sounded perfect to him. Then he wouldn't feel guilty if the topic of business came up on a date. It wouldn't seem like he was trying to get free advice in a social situation.

That was why he'd come into her office ASAP, so she

wouldn't ever think he was trying to take advantage of their relationship to get PR help for nothing. He was confused about her attitude, though. Apparently she'd been interested enough in the project to mention it to her boss this morning, and yet a few minutes ago she'd tried to turn his account over to her friend Gretchen.

"Retainer, then." She typed that into her computer. "I'll need your numbers—work, home, fax, cell."

"I can't believe I didn't give you all that yesterday." He took a business card out of his wallet and slid it across the desk. "That's another reason I came in. I realized you couldn't call me because you didn't have any of this information."

She scooted the card closer and filled in the little boxes on her screen. "Okay, then." Swinging back around, she faced him with all the eagerness of a mourner at a wake. "We need to do some preliminary work before I can outline a potential campaign for your approval. I can either ask you the questions now, or give you a questionnaire to fill out."

He leaned in a little closer. "Kasey, why don't you want to do this?"

"Of course I want to do this." Her jaw was rigid.

"No, you don't. And I need to understand why. Can we go get some coffee and talk about it?"

She looked wary. "Where?"

"I was thinking Coco's down the street." He'd love to take her home with him, but that might get her into trouble.

"Um, maybe that's a good idea."

"Then let's go." He waited for her to grab her briefcase, although she left her suit jacket hanging on the back of her chair as if to signal that she was coming back shortly.

Obviously she was a very conscientious worker, and he'd respect that. He paused by the front door while she spoke to the receptionist, a woman named Myra. Myra had been very nice to him when he'd arrived, much more welcoming than Kasey, come to think of it. Myra smiled at Kasey as if they shared some sort of secret. Maybe they did, because as Kasey turned and walked toward him, she was blushing.

"All I have is my truck," he said as they left the office and headed for the elevator.

"That's fine."

He thought of her climbing into his truck in that short skirt and hoped he'd be able to control himself. A gentleman would help a lady up in a situation like that, but hoisting Kasey onto the seat could create a host of problems for him. He'd have to think about dissecting frogs again.

Although they passed a couple of people in the hall, they had the elevator to themselves. Sam kept his distance, not wanting to start something he couldn't finish, but at least he could speak freely now. "I really am sorry that we were rushed this morning," he said. "When two people have shared as much as we did, they should have a chance to talk to each other before they go on about their day."

Her expression had closed down again. "Maybe that was for the best."

"Why would that be for the best?"

"Because now you're a client."

He didn't like the way she said that, as if he'd contracted a contagious disease. The elevator opened and he ushered her into the lobby. "And your point is?"

"I'll explain over coffee." Then she turned a smile on two businessmen coming through the front door of the building. "Good morning!"

They both greeted her in return, and Sam felt like a little boy who'd been chastised for talking during class. Once they were outside the building, he told her that.

"I just don't want my colleagues to get the idea that I have a personal relationship with a client." She put on her sunglasses.

"Why not?" Sliding on his own shades, he led the way to the parking lot, reaching for his keys as he walked.

"It's unprofessional."

"Oh, come on. Are you saying that if your dear uncle Morty wanted to hire you to do PR work, you'd refuse because you already know him?"

"That's not the same thing."

"Sure, it is." As they approached the passenger side of his truck, he clicked the button on his key chain and unlocked the door. "And I'm paying the retainer, so that simplifies our interaction, don't you think?"

"No."

He sighed. This was getting very complicated, but she was worth it. He opened the door. "I'll need to help you in."

"I can do it." She stepped up on the running board. Then she turned to him. "Go ahead and get in. I can make it."

They gazed at each other in silence. Finally he shrugged and walked around the truck. No doubt she could climb in just fine without him. He supposed he'd secretly wanted to help her because he would get to touch her, but he was out of luck.

She'd certainly turned into a prim and proper businesswoman today. He had a tough time believing she was the same person who had boogied on the dance floor and rubbed her body against his, the same person who had agreed to lie nearly naked in a hammock while he...

He groaned and shook his head. Thinking about that wasn't such a good idea. He could feel the repercussions of such thoughts as he stepped up into the truck cab. By the time he got behind the wheel she was already in with her door closed and her seat belt fastened.

"I'll put the air on. It's warm in here." He started the engine and punched a button to turn the air conditioner on high. If only he had a similar switch so he could turn himself off. Sitting with Kasey in the close confines of this truck reminded him of how much fun they'd had the night before. And he wanted to continue along those lines.

"Is Coco's all right with you?" he asked. *How about the nearest hotel room?*

"Coco's is fine."

"Then Coco's it is." He put the truck in gear and drove out of the parking lot, all the while trying to ignore the sexy woman in the passenger seat. He failed. Her perfume filled the cab of his truck and he was so sensitized to her that he could hear every breath, every rustle of clothing.

"You know, if my being a client makes you that uptight, we can forget that part," he said. "It's just that I think you could help me, and I don't trust anyone else to do the job. But I also don't want to ruin what we have going."

"You should probably—" She coughed and cleared her throat. "You should probably let me do your PR work for you. If your business grows, that will be good for you and good for your brother."

"I think that's all true, but something's happened to the connection we made last night. If the PR work is interfering, then I want to—"

"You passed Coco's."

"Whoops." He hung a U and drove back to the restaurant. "Anyway, as I was saying, our relationship is important to me." He turned into the parking lot and found a space near the door. "I don't want this idea I had for my business to cause problems between us."

"Sam, we would have had problems, regardless."

"We would?" An icy finger tickled his spine. Instead of turning off the engine, he put the gearshift in neutral and pulled on the emergency brake so he could leave the motor running and the air on. Then he unfastened his seat belt and turned to her. Whatever she had to say, he didn't want a restaurant table between them when she said it. "How come?"

She took off her sunglasses and looked at him, her expression sad. "We're at different places in our lives. You just bought a house, while I still live in an apartment, an apartment I haven't even bothered to decorate."

"Does that matter?" So maybe he shouldn't have given her a tour. "I don't care whether your apartment is decorated or not, Kasey. Maybe I gave you the wrong idea about me. I'm not obsessed about the whole house thing." *But I am becoming obsessed about you, wondering when I'll be able to kiss you again, and do other things.*

"Maybe we should consider last night a fun experiment, something we'll both remember fondly."

"Remember fondly?" He started to panic. "Look, I shouldn't have allowed us to oversleep. That wasn't smooth, and I apologize, but—"

"This has nothing to do with the oversleeping."

"Then what's the problem?" He took off his shades so he could see her expression better and she could see his. "You had a good time last night. I know you did. Or were you faking those orgasms?"

Her voice trembled slightly. "No, I wasn't."

"So you liked what I was doing."

"Yes."

"Then what happened? What did I do to turn you off? Am I some snore machine? Did I—"

"No, no, no! It's not you! It's me! I'm not ready for this kind of intensity, that's all."

He stared at her. So that was it. She was simply a good-time girl who'd enjoyed their sexual adventures and wanted a no-strings situation. On the other hand, he was coming on as a guy interested in a commitment of some kind. He'd taken her through his house, and she'd assumed he was casting her in some permanent role in his life. He wasn't...yet.

Apparently he had a skittish woman on his hands. He'd been in this situation before with Veronica, who had been too young to make a commitment. After handling that poorly, he didn't want to repeat the mistake and push Kasey into leaving.

He'd assumed she was close to his age, but maybe not. He could ask her, but that could backfire by emphasizing their differences. Maybe he should just let her go, but after what they'd shared the night before, he couldn't bring himself to walk away.

"All right." He took a deep breath. "All things considered, I can see why you'd think I want to tie you down. The truth is, I took you back to my house because I knew we'd have privacy there and that would make the sex better. But we could have gone to your place."

She swallowed. "I, um, got the impression this was about more than sex."

"Sorry if I implied that. This is very much about sex." He reached over and slipped his hand beneath her hair to cup the nape of her neck. "I want you, Kasey. I'm intense about that—I'll admit it. If I thought we could get away with having sex right here in the parking lot, I'd suggest it. From the way you acted last night, I thought you felt the same."

"I did, but—"

"But if I'm looking for a steady roommate, you're not that girl. Am I right?"

"Yes, you're right."

"Then let me put your mind at ease." He proceeded to lie through his teeth. "I'm not looking for a steady roommate." He massaged the back of her neck and felt her quiver. He was probably a sucker for trying to nurture something that had all the signs of being a repeat of his relationship with Veronica, but Veronica hadn't turned him inside out in the space of twenty-four hours. Kasey had. "I am looking for more amazing nights like we had last night," he said, and that much was true.

Heat flashed in her eyes. "But you're...you're a client."

"Want me to cancel that arrangement?"

"No. That makes no sense. I can't have you scuttling your whole plan because you want to have sex with me. There's also the little problem of Beckworth. I'd have to explain why I lost you as a client. I can certainly figure out some way to do that, but—"

"But why do it at all? Think win-win, Kasey. How about this? I'll stay completely out of your office. No one has to see us together. We'll work in private and play in private. You'll take care of the account and no one has to know that we're having mind-blowing sex at the same time. That will be our little secret."

Her breathing quickened. "I don't know...."

"I promise you, we'll be very careful."

"So you really won't tell anyone? Not even your friends?"

"No one. I won't drag you into my life and you won't make me part of yours. We'll just be getting together to discuss the PR campaign and have great sex." Although that wasn't the way he would have preferred it, he could tell the concept excited her. Now if only his suggestion was convincing enough to get her back into his bed. "What do you think?"

"I think you'd better take me back to the office."

His heart sank. "That's a no?"

She smiled. "It's a yes. And if you don't take me back

to work immediately, I might jump you right here, which would blow our cover."

KASEY KNEW she was taking a huge risk, but if Sam kept his word, she might get away with having more sex with him and still not reveal her age or her identity. And she wanted to have more sex with him. Just sitting in this truck while he caressed the back of her neck was driving her crazy.

"All right, I'll take you back to the office." His smile was slow and sensual. "And somehow I'll control myself and not kiss you right now, which I really, really want to do."

"That would be a bad idea. We have to act as if we have no sexual interest in each other at all."

"That will be a trick, considering how much I want to strip you naked and lick your—"

"Sam, take me back to the office. Now." Heat flowed through her, dampening her panties and making her tremble.

He sighed and stopped stroking her neck. Then he turned and buckled his seat belt. "I'm not a patient man. How soon can I see you again?"

She loved his sense of urgency, especially now that he'd promised her it would lead to nothing permanent. Thinking about having sex with him again made her weak with lust. "I have this...thing to go to tonight."

"When can you get away?" He left the parking lot and drove down the street toward her office building.

She quickly calculated time and distance. If she left work soon after five, she could be at her mother's— even factoring in rush hour—by six-thirty, when the basket party was due to start. She'd put in her order and leave. The return should be much quicker. "I'll be free by eight-thirty," she said.

"Your place or mine?"

"Mine. An apartment complex is more anonymous. I'm afraid your neighbors might start to recognize me. My neighbors don't pay that much attention to the comings and goings of the tenants."

"We could find a way around my neighbors, but I'd be glad to come to your place. I would come to a tent in the middle of the desert if you'd let me use my tongue to—"

"How do you expect me to get any work done today if you leave me with that kind of image?"

He laughed. "I *want* to leave you with that kind of image. You're so damned dedicated to your job that I need to make sure you'll still want me when I show up at your apartment tonight."

There was no danger that she wouldn't want him. He had no idea how potent he was, and how tempted she'd been to throw all caution to the wind so that she could be with him. Fortunately he'd taken her protests seriously and created a situation where she felt relatively safe.

Now, even if he followed through on his idea of contacting her brother, he wouldn't mention the woman he was having hot sex with. He wouldn't discuss it with his own brother or with anyone. Neither would she. The girls in the office might guess, but they wouldn't know anything for sure. Maybe being mysterious was the best Bad Girl tactic of all.

In any case, she'd have a chance to find out if last

night with Sam had been a fluke, or if she really was capable of being multiorgasmic. She'd find out if Sam could be as imaginative in her apartment setting as he'd been on his back patio, and if she had any creative ideas of her own on the subject of sex. Yes, continuing this fling with Sam could be dangerous, but the potential rewards were so exciting she couldn't resist.

11

KASEY HAD A HARD TIME getting away from the basket party. Most of her mother's friends hadn't seen her since her makeover, and they kept her locked in conversation as they commented on how different she looked. At least she was no longer treated like little Kasey Braddock, girl genius. The image had weighed her down all her life and she was glad to be rid of it.

Except now, instead of fawning over her brains, the women zeroed in on her social life. So this was how it had been for the popular girls, she thought. Not so much better than being a brain, really. Having her mom's friends ask about her dates felt very strange, especially considering what her activities had been the night before and what they promised to be again tonight. On her way home from her mother's house she planned to buy condoms.

And she couldn't very well say she'd won an office lottery for the privilege of hitting on Sam. The idea would scandalize her mother, and besides, Sam was her secret, and she was his—at least she hoped to hell he would keep quiet about their liaison. So she smiled at the ladies buying baskets and deflected the questions about boyfriends. Then she ordered her mother's birthday present, gave everyone a hug and finally escaped.

By driving like a maniac on the way home and buying condoms in record time, she arrived at her apartment with twenty minutes to spare. She changed clothes quickly and tidied the bedroom, remembering to stash all family pictures in a dresser drawer. Then she walked into her living room and was hit by an attack of nerves.

Compared to Sam's house, her place wasn't much. She'd put all her spare cash into her top priorities—a salon visit once every two weeks, a new wardrobe and a zippy little convertible. Her apartment hadn't seemed important, because she didn't invite men over to visit.

Until now. Glancing around, she groaned in despair. Tacky furniture, half-dead plant, zero ambience except for the vase of roses, courtesy of Sam. She should have thought of chilling some wine and lighting some candles. Wait—she had candles! All she had to do was find them.

Five minutes later, she'd torn through every kitchen drawer and located two boxes of candles, one red and one green. Someone had given them to her for Christmas two years ago and she'd never used them. After suffering through a summer in her apartment, they weren't exactly ruler straight, but they were all she had.

Then she remembered why she'd never used the candles—no candleholders. Whoever had given them to her must have assumed that everyone owned candleholders. Kasey didn't. But she'd started on this candlelight kick and she'd figure it out.

By the time Sam rang her doorbell, she had eight tapers burning in her apartment—two in the kitchen, two in the living room, three in the bedroom and one in the bathroom. She'd turned off all the lights, and what everyone said about candlelight was true. The apartment looked tons better. Even her ratty furniture had taken on a romantic glow. Drawing in a deep breath, she opened her door.

Sam stood there holding another dozen roses, white this time, and a long-necked bottle in a paper bag. "Hey, Kasey." He swept her with a glance, his eyes hungry.

"More roses!" The heat in his eyes made her heart race. As she accepted the tissue-wrapped bouquet, she looked down at her khaki shorts and white tank top. "Now I feel underdressed for the occasion."

"Or overdressed," he said suggestively as he walked in. "As far as I'm concerned, you could have come to the door wearing a smile."

Would she have dared? Probably not, but a more sophisticated woman might have, and she didn't want him to know the thought hadn't even crossed her mind. "I didn't want to make everything too easy for you," she murmured.

Excitement gleamed in his eyes. "Challenges can be stimulating, too." Then he cupped her head in one hand and kissed her.

The magnitude of that kiss made her long to toss the roses to the floor and drag him off to the bedroom, but that wouldn't be cool. She was having a grown-up affair and she wanted to conduct herself as if she knew the routine.

Slowly he lifted his lips from hers. "Let's get rid of the roses and the champagne so our hands are free."

Then again, she might not have to worry about being a grown-up. How nice. "You brought champagne?"

"Yeah." He lifted the bottle. "For later."

"Are we celebrating something?"

"Absolutely." He glanced around. "Nice effect with the candles, by the way."

"Thank you." She wondered if he'd notice that she'd used masking tape to hold the candles inside little juice glasses. Now she had to figure out what to put the roses in. Her only vase was currently in use.

"I'll go find something for the roses," she said, planning to dream up a solution on her way into the kitchen.

"I'll come with you."

"That's okay. I'll be back before you know it." She really didn't want him to watch while she rummaged through her meager supply of kitchen stuff.

But he followed her, anyway. "I'm not letting you out of my sight, lady. I've been waiting all day to be with you, and I'm not wasting a single second. I can put the champagne in the refrigerator while you take care of the roses."

"Um, all right." So he'd watch her rummage. At least she'd be rummaging by candlelight. "So what are we celebrating?" she asked as they walked into the tiny space barely big enough for a sink and appliances. In her experience, champagne was saved for engagements, weddings and anniversaries.

"Another night of great sex."

Her heart leaped into her throat, but she tried to appear casual, tried to stop trembling with lust and anticipation. She turned to smile at him. "You're that sure it will be?"

"Would I bring champagne otherwise?" He pulled the bottle out of the bag.

"Oh, the pressure."

"I'm sure you can handle it." He waggled his eyebrows. "I'm sure you can handle everything very capably, as people kept saying this morning."

She rolled her eyes. "Now there was an embarrassing moment, my boss saying I had capable hands and you rushing to agree with him."

"He had no idea that I was talking about something besides your PR work."

"No, but *I* did. You wanted to get me flustered."

"Who, me?" He tried to look innocent and failed miserably.

"It's a good thing you're not coming in there anymore. Honestly, what were you thinking?"

"I can't think when you're around. That's the problem. All the blood drains south and I turn into a randy teenager with only sex on the brain."

She couldn't help laughing. "You're crazy."

"About getting naked with you, yes, I am." He opened the refrigerator and laid the bottle on its side on the top shelf.

All this talk about sex wasn't helping her come up with a solution for the roses. She went through her cabinets, hoping a crystal vase would somehow materialize. All she found were water glasses. Even if she divided the roses and put them in the glasses, the glasses would tip over.

She had one thing that would hold them—her popcorn bowl—but they'd have to lie sideways in it. Finally, with a sigh of resignation, she pulled it from a bottom shelf. "Behold my flower vase."

He leaned against the counter and grinned at her. "Interesting. You must not be much of a pack rat. I'll bet you've had a gazillion flower deliveries in the past few years."

"Oh, not so much." She ran water in the popcorn bowl and unwrapped the roses.

"Are you telling me that guys have been that intimidated by your brains?"

Yes. But she didn't want to appear pathetically under-dated. "It's possible I'm just choosy." She laid the roses in the bowl, resting the stems on the edge. Maybe she'd start a new flower-arranging trend with this look.

"You should be choosy." He closed the small distance between them and reached for her. "An incredible woman like you should have her pick."

She abandoned the roses to snuggle happily into his arms. With Sam, she felt like that kind of woman. This morning he'd begged her to let him see her again. A hundred times today she'd replayed that scene in the Coco's parking lot, impressed that she'd brought him to that state.

He pulled her in close, close enough to make his arousal obvious. "I don't mean to be pushy, but the flowers are in water and the champagne's in the fridge."

As her blood heated even more, she wound her arms around his neck. His implication that they should move on to other activities made her shiver with longing. "Would you like a tour of my apartment?"

"Yes."

"Then come with me." She slipped out of his arms and took his hand.

"Don't you think we should blow out the candles before we start the tour?"

"Oh." She glanced at the ten-inch tapers, which hadn't even burned down an inch yet.

"We'd better blow them out." Sam walked over to the counter and doused both flames. "And the ones in the living room, too." He turned to her. "I assume the tour of your apartment begins in your bedroom?"

She wanted him so much her mouth was watering. "Uh-huh."

"In that case, by the time we remembered the candles, we might have burned the house down."

SAM WAS DEVELOPING a fondness for Kasey's endearing lack of sophistication when it came to housewares. She had one cheap vase and no candleholders, judging from the juice-glass-and-masking-tape combo she'd used to support the candles. Even the swaybacked candles had seen better days. Yet he could see her clever mind at work in creating the holders, and she'd attempted to give her place atmosphere. He found that touching.

Obviously she didn't know that he'd built up such a case of lust for her that atmosphere was wasted on him. As far as he was concerned, they could be anywhere as long as there was a surface that would hold their weight. He ached for her, and nothing mattered except stripping off their clothes and getting horizontal. Actually, vertical would work, too.

In fact, this hallway she was leading him down would be fine, up against the wall or braced against a doorjamb or on the carpeted floor, for that matter. He was a desperate man with a rocket in his pocket. But maybe he needed to pull back and not appear so needy. He'd scared her off before. He didn't want to do that again.

She had the masking-tape-and-juice-glass candle arrangement going on in her bedroom, too. In the light from three flickering tapers he saw a double bed with the covers turned down. He liked imagining her in this room a little while ago, folding back the covers and thinking about what they'd do together on the bed.

A double meant less room to roll around, but it was cozier, in a way. He didn't mind a double bed. He wouldn't mind a sleeping bag thrown on the ground. Beside the bed were a lamp and nightstands of the same vintage as her living-room furniture.

He might ask her to turn the lamp on before the night was over. She was so beautiful, and he wanted another chance to enjoy the view. He wanted many chances. There were blinds over each of her windows, even in the living room and kitchen. Maybe he could talk her into drinking champagne naked.

"This is it." She led him into the room. "Nothing fancy."

"Are you kidding?" He nudged off his shoes as he edged her toward the soft expanse of her bed. "You make any bed fancy."

"I don't have a king-size mattress."

"The better to find you, my dear." He pulled her down to the bed and rolled on top of her. "See? Got-

cha." Oh, man, this was heaven. With his package nestled between her thighs, he started working her out of
her tank top.

"And I have neighbors on the other side of this
wall."

"Have they ever complained?" He pushed her top
up over the lacy cups of her bra. Yes, he wanted some
of that.

"No."

He was so captivated by the way her breasts swelled
beneath the white lace of her bra that her answer took a
while to register. He looked into her eyes. "No? You've
been that careful not to make noise?"

"I don't make noise."

"Oh, yes, you do. You may think you don't, but I've
been there, and you definitely make noise. If you've
had an orgasm in this bed, I venture to say the neighbors are aware of it."

She simply looked up at him and said nothing.

At last a possibility dawned on him. "No orgasms in
this bed?"

Even in the dim light from the candles, her blush
showed. "Not that kind."

"I'm not sure what you mean." Then he figured it
out. "Oh. I guess when you make yourself come, you
can control the noise level better."

"Uh-huh."

"You're blushing." He thought that was the cutest
thing, a new-millennium woman who was a little bit
embarrassed about the subject of masturbation.

"I can't help it. I've never talked about this subject
with a guy."

"Good. I want you to talk about it with me." He was enormously pleased to discover something he could share with her that no other man had. "But first raise your arms so I can get rid of this tank top."

"We don't have to talk about it." She lifted her arms so he could pull the top over her head.

"But I would love to." He threw the piece of clothing on the floor and slid both hands under her back, groping for the fastening of her bra. That was another thing about her that intrigued him. Most women into seduction wore front-clasp bras, but Kasey hadn't picked up on that trick. He sort of liked that she hadn't.

"Why would you want to talk about it?"

"Because." He unhooked her bra and got that off. With a sigh of delight he gazed at her. His memory had served him well, but he'd forgotten the sweet little freckle right there, on the underside of her left breast. He leaned down to kiss it and she quivered.

So did he. Her skin was so soft. Although he intended to continue the promising discussion they'd recently left, first he needed to spend some time honoring her spectacular breasts. His penis throbbed, reminding him of what he ultimately had to have, but he thought he could hold off a little while longer. And her breasts invited him to play. He really hadn't had his fill the night before.

Propping himself on one arm, he caressed her, lifting and massaging her breasts while he listened to her breathing change. "When you masturbate, do you touch yourself here?" he asked.

"Um..."

"I'll bet you do." He stared into her eyes, which

grew darker the longer he caressed her. But she still wore her blue contacts. Before the night was over, he'd coax her to take them out, so he could see the true color of her eyes. "Come on, 'fess up. You play with your breasts."

Her eyelashes fluttered. "Maybe."

"You do. I know it, because you like it when I touch you there."

"Uh...huh."

"But here's something you can't do for yourself." He cradled the weight of her breast in his hand and leaned down to feather a kiss over her nipple. The firm tip reminded him of a plump raspberry. He liked raspberries, but he'd take this treat over an entire bowlful. He drew her nipple in, then rolled it gently against the roof of his mouth and was rewarded with her soft moan.

Then he began to suck, loving the sensation, loving the taste of her and the flowery scent swirling around him. She moaned again and arched her hips. Much as he wanted to unzip both his pants and her shorts and take her right then, he had another agenda that would teach him more about Kasey. He wanted to know her better than anyone.

Releasing her breast with great reluctance, he rolled to his side. Now he had full access to her. He reached for the button on her shorts, unfastened it and pulled down the zipper. When he took them off, he deliberately left her panties in place.

"I have... I have condoms," she said in a husky voice.

"Me, too." He'd stashed several in his pocket, not

willing to take a chance they'd be without. "You can never have too many."

Her answering laughter sounded breathless. "Guess not."

He slid his hand inside her panties. He had an idea, something that would excite him tremendously, but he didn't think she'd do it unless he left her panties on.

She was slick and hot, and his pulse hammered as he stroked downward, curving his middle finger so he could probe inside. "Is this how you do it?" He moved his finger slowly, knowing from the way her breath caught that she wasn't too far from a climax.

"I...sort of."

He pulled his hand back. "Show me."

She shook her head, but her eyes glowed with excitement.

"I want to see. Please."

"I...can't."

"Sure you can. Like this." He eased his hand under the waistband of her panties again and found her hot spot. "I would love to see how you make yourself come."

She groaned. "Please...just..."

"Do it for me." Once again he pulled his hand away. "I want..."

"I know. You want to come. Make it happen. Show me."

She caught her lower lip between her teeth. Then she closed her eyes. Slowly, tentatively she slid her hand down over her stomach. After a slight hesitation, she worked her hand under the elastic band.

He would give anything to watch this when she was

naked, but that might take some time and patience. He'd be grateful for this small concession, something she'd never done for another man. His heart pumped wildly as her hand, outlined by the smooth satin of her panties, began to move in a rhythmic way. With her other hand she stroked her breast and pinched her nipple.

Damn, he'd better be careful or he'd come right along with her.

Her lips parted and she gasped. Her movements grew quicker, and then she arched upward with a muted cry.

Sam watched through a haze of desire. He'd never wanted another woman this much, which told him Kasey could be the one he needed to share his life with. And she'd asked for a no-strings affair. Somehow, someday, he had to convince her otherwise.

12

BY THE TIME Kasey opened her eyes, she'd changed. The shy girl who'd been embarrassed to masturbate in front of a lover had left the building. In her place lay a sexual woman who enjoyed giving herself the extra thrill of having Sam watch. And now she was ready to make her own desires known.

Slowly she peeled off her panties. "Well? Did you like that?"

His voice rasped in the stillness. "Yes."

"Now it's my turn for a fantasy." She sat up. "I want you to lie on your back."

"Why—" He paused to clear his throat. "Why do you want me to do that?"

"I want to play. And all the interesting toys are in the front." Ideas came to her like lightning. She knew how she affected Sam. So she'd put him through his paces and revel in her power.

"All right." He kept his attention on her as he stretched out. "Clothes on or off?"

"I'll worry about that." She climbed off the bed. "I'll be right back."

"Where are you going?"

"You'll see." Discarding her first thought, which was to grab her bathrobe out of the closet, she walked down the hall and through the living room with nothing on. She'd never done that in her life. Tonight it felt perfect.

She went into the kitchen and flicked on a light. Once she'd opened the refrigerator, she snagged a can of whipped cream and padded back across the kitchen. To think that when she'd bought the whipped cream she'd intended to put it on the chocolate pie she'd brought home from the bakery. Wait a minute—the chocolate pie might come in handy, too.

Doing an about-face, she returned to the refrigerator and took out the pie. Sam might have a hammock in a private little patio, but she had whipped cream and a chocolate pie. The neighbors were liable to get an earful, but that couldn't be helped. That was apartment living for you. She turned out the kitchen light and headed back to the bedroom...and Sam.

On the way back down the hall, she called out to him, "Here I come."

His voice sounded a little bit strained. "How do you mean that, exactly?"

She laughed. "In the nonsexual sense, this time. This next episode will be about you, not me." She walked through the doorway and noticed from the jut of his fly that the flag was definitely up on his mailbox. "Just don't start without me, okay?"

His eyes widened. "Whipped cream?"

"Oh, yeah. And chocolate pie. I missed dessert tonight." She'd missed dinner, too, but who cared?

"Uh...I see."

"Maybe you're beginning to. First rule, I'm in charge." She sat beside him on the bed and put the whipped cream and pie on the nightstand.

"You walked naked through your apartment." With a smile, he reached out to cup her swaying breast.

She batted his hand away. "No touching me. I get to touch you, now. And yes, I walked naked through my apartment. What of it?"

"I'll bet you've never done that before."

"Maybe not."

"How did it feel?"

"Good." She began unbuttoning his shirt. "Now hold still."

"I can't promise a thing."

"Then hold as still as you can." She tugged his shirt from the waistband of his slacks and spread it open. "There." He had such a great chest, lightly furred with dark hair and muscled enough to be manly without the overdeveloped physique of a professional body-builder. It was no wonder the women at Beckworth had spent most of the day watching him trim the mesquite tree.

Now she had the privilege of enjoying his body all by herself. Gretchen had tried to get her to spill the details of her relationship with Sam, but Kasey had claimed they were only friends. She'd told Gretchen that Sam was now a client and she shouldn't get involved with a client anyway. Gretchen had protested that this particular client would be worth breaking a few rules for.

Gazing down at Sam, Kasey had to agree with Gretchen. Smoothing her hands down his chest, she gazed into his eyes and watched them darken in reaction to her touch. Then she stroked his arms and lingered on his tattoo. "Why did you get this?" She traced the pattern lightly with one finger.

"In high school I had a reputation for being too nice."

"I can believe that." She brushed her palms over his nipples.

"I thought... I thought a big bad tattoo would help my rep."

She smiled. He was definitely getting more aroused with every caress. "And did it help your rep?"

"Oh, yeah. Instant tough guy."

"I'll bet." She leaned over him and nibbled on his lower lip. "By the way, I have neighbors, but don't worry about making noise."

"I can control it."

She trailed kisses along his jaw until her lips were right next to his ear. "We'll see." Then she gently nipped his earlobe. "We'll see about that, tough guy." Then she sat up and reached for the can of whipped cream.

SAM WAS FASCINATED by the transformation in Kasey. From the evidence, she'd passed some milestone by making herself come while he looked on. He'd meant to nudge her a little further down the road of sensuality. Apparently he'd launched her onto the superhighway of sexual adventure.

He wasn't complaining, but he would have to keep his wits about him if he intended to stay in the game. With her brains, she could outpace him in the innovation department in no time. And he was very much afraid that if she ever got bored, she'd be gone.

She wasn't bored yet, however, because she'd just discovered whipped cream. He gasped when she squirted a mound of the cold white stuff on his nipple. He hadn't thought that his nipples were overly sensitive, but when she started lapping at the whipped cream with her warm tongue, he changed his mind. She licked him clean before zapping the other side. Wild.

Incredible how her attention to that one little spot had him going. And he knew exactly what other target she had in mind for that squirt can. But he wasn't quite sure what she planned to do with the pie, or whether he'd survive it without coming in a very loud and spectacular fashion.

He knew that was her goal, to prove that she could make him lose all control and yell like a banshee. Because he wanted to continue to challenge her, he would fight like hell not to do what she expected. He sensed that the unexpected would keep her interested, and he very much wanted to keep her interested.

When she finished playing with his nipples, she took off his pants and briefs. He was supposed to lie there and let her undress him, and that was a whole new experience, too, because she wasn't very practiced at it. She fumbled around a lot and kept laughing and brushing her naked body against him. When she bumped his aching penis with her breast, he nearly erupted from that single contact.

"Are we having fun, yet?" she asked once she'd pulled off his slacks and briefs and dropped them on the floor. "How're you doing down here?" She wrapped her fingers around his shaft.

"Terrific." He clenched his jaw against the release that pounded at the gates of his self-control, begging him to surrender. He knew she'd pick up that whipped-cream can again, and he wondered how he'd make it through another tongue bath, especially if it involved that rebellious part of his anatomy she held in her hand.

But instead of the whipped cream, she picked up the pie. His brain stalled just thinking of the possibilities. Here he'd been hoping that before the night was over, she'd drink champagne naked. In the past half hour, she'd shot right past that mark and was on to more creative turn-ons.

"Do you like chocolate pie?" she asked.

"Sure."

"Me, too." She stuck two fingers into the center of the pie and lifted out a glob of chocolate filling.

He fully expected it to end up on some part of him, but instead she started licking it off her fingers.

"This is very good." She put both fingers in her mouth and sucked on them. Then she scooped up another glob and repeated the process.

He began to understand her devious plan. She was playing mind games with him, letting him watch her lick and suck her fingers while he imagined what she could do to his penis.

"Want some?" She extended her hand, a quivering bit of chocolate filling on her fingertips.

"Love some." He tried to pretend that he wasn't lying there completely erect and that she didn't have him right where she wanted him. He sucked the chocolate off her fingers and used his tongue to clean off every last morsel. Two could play at this game.

She definitely responded to the movement of his

tongue. Her breathing quickened as she watched him slide it right between her fingers. "Want more?" she murmured.

"Sure." He met her gaze. There was plenty of filling in that pie. Enough for him to have a little fun, too. He took his time getting the chocolate off her fingers when she gave him a second helping. He sucked on her middle finger a little longer than was necessary, and noticed her shiver.

"Let's try something else," she said, and her voice trembled, revealing that she wasn't in complete control.

"Whatever you want."

"Let's see how this feels." And she smeared the filling over the tip of his penis.

He moaned. Couldn't help it. The cool, creamy texture against his hot, tight shaft drove him insane. He clutched the sheets beneath him, closing his hands into fists as his muscles bunched, wanting that climax more than life itself.

Then she began to lick.

He didn't last very long. "Kasey..." He writhed against the mattress. "Kasey, I'm... I can't stop..."

"Go ahead," she murmured, right before she slid her mouth down over him and sucked hard.

Oh, he made noise all right. All his macho pride went right out the window as he climaxed. He told the world about it, made sure everyone in the next county knew that he'd come. And when it was over, he lay panting, his eyes closed, his body drained of every last bit of energy.

He felt the moment when she released him, felt the silken slide of her body as she moved up the mattress.

Then she nuzzled his ear and nipped his earlobe again. "Gotcha," she whispered.

KASEY LAY DOWN next to Sam, put her hands behind her head and gazed at the dancing shadows created by the candle flame. So this was what sexual liberation was like. She'd always wondered if she had the necessary temperament to be a wild woman. Sam had helped her answer that question.

Even though they'd eventually have to part ways, she'd always be grateful to him. Maybe she'd needed someone older to guide her through this. A less experienced man might not have gently pushed her to explore her options.

What a good time she'd had with the whipped cream and the pie. The only unintended side effect was her own arousal. She wondered if Sam would drift off to sleep and leave her to deal with that on her own. If he did, then she would. He'd taught her to take what she wanted.

And she did ache for another climax. Being with Sam had cranked up her libido, and now one orgasm wasn't nearly enough. She glanced over at him and saw that his eyes were still closed. She'd worked him pretty hard the past two nights. He probably needed his rest.

Slowly she reached between her legs, where she was very hot and wet. Yes, she needed to come again, maybe even twice. She hadn't understood herself before, but the fact was, she was a highly sexed woman. And a highly sexed woman needed satisfaction.

"Can I help?"

With her hand still in position, she turned her head and found that he'd rolled to his side and was watching her. "That's up to you."

His chuckle was low and intimate. "What progress. You'd give me a repeat performance, wouldn't you?"

"Or I can let you sleep. Maybe you need to relax and take it easy."

His eyebrows lifted. "Oh? Are you questioning my stamina?"

"You seem kind of...wiped out."

"Well, I've recovered." He circled her wrist with his fingers and lifted her hand, guiding it to his mouth. "And hungry." He licked her damp fingers.

She quivered, remembering the scene in the hammock the night before. That might have been the true beginning of her transformation. No man had ever given her such unparalleled pleasure. Sam had elevated oral sex to an art form.

He nuzzled her palm. "Do you like chocolate pie with or without whipped cream?"

She gulped. "That depends."

"I'm not sure which I want, either." Releasing her hand, he shrugged out of his shirt. "Lift up."

"Why?" She thought she knew, and her blood ran hot.

"You had your turn. Now I want to play. Lift up."

When she raised her hips off the bed, he shoved his folded shirt underneath her. Then he reached for the pie and the can of whipped cream. "Choices, choices."

Her heart beat faster as he got up from the bed and walked around to the foot, surveying her the entire time. Not long ago she would have felt vulnerable and exposed if a man had done that. Now she was proud of her body, proud of how completely she'd captured his attention.

At last he nodded. "I have a taste for both chocolate and whipped cream. I've found the perfect spot to enjoy it, and I want to be comfortable, so we need a small adjustment." After laying the pie and the can of whipped cream on the end of the bed, he leaned over it and grasped her thighs.

"Sam! What—" But she understood when he scooted her, shirt and all, closer to the end of the bed.

"Now hold still," he said, a smile in his voice as he repeated her instructions.

"Yeah, right." Her voice shook. "Like you stayed still while I did this." She lifted her head.

"Maybe you're stronger than I was." He sank to his knees at the foot of the bed.

"Maybe." She doubted it, especially considering what he had in store for her. She let her head fall back to the mattress.

"First, a little chocolate filling."

She thought she was prepared, but even so, she gasped as the cool substance settled over her hot vulva. The sensation was arousing in a way she never would have imagined. So this was what she'd let him in for a while ago.

And he wanted to return the favor. No, he wanted to up the ante. Whipped cream under pressure danced across her trigger point, making her moan with pleasure.

"Ah. I think we need more of that." He licked it

away, which only drove her wilder. Then he hit her with another spurt, cleaned her off with his tongue and tried it again.

She began to tremble violently, closing in on her climax.

"Now for the chocolate," he murmured, and began lapping, finishing each stroke by paying special attention to the area he'd zapped with whipped cream.

She'd never felt anything like it. Almost without warning, an orgasm ripped through her, forcing cries of ecstasy from her throat. But he wasn't finished. He stroked on more chocolate and kept going. She was in for an incredible ride.

This time he had to hold her steady while he licked, because she thrashed around, driven out of her mind by his clever tongue and the powerful undulations that rolled through her again and again. One climax blended into another as she gasped and bucked in his arms.

When at last he eased her back to the mattress, she was sobbing with gratitude, totally wrung out with the force of her body's response. Her ears rang and every nerve quivered. She was his puppet, his slave. Had he asked her to run away with him, to give up everything to be with him and make love every waking moment, she would have done it.

Instead he crawled up beside her and gathered her quaking body close to his. Carefully he brushed her hair back from her ear and placed his lips there. "Gotcha," he whispered.

13

AFTER THE CHOCOLATE-PIE-and-whipped-cream incident, Sam had no problem persuading Kasey to walk naked into the kitchen with him so they could break out the champagne. "See, I told you we'd have something to celebrate," he said as he opened the refrigerator and pulled out the bottle. It wasn't Dom Pérignon, because he hadn't wanted to be too flashy, but it was a decent brand.

"You did tell me that." She set a couple of inexpensive wineglasses on the counter. "I guess you've figured out by now that I don't have a lot of the amenities."

He unscrewed the wire from the plastic cap on the champagne. "Lady, you have chocolate pie and a can of whipped cream. The amenities don't get any better than that."

"That was pure accident." Then she seemed to catch herself. "I mean, I knew they might come in handy, but I wasn't sure how you'd react if I suggested something that wild."

"Oh, come on." He laughed as he grabbed a kitchen towel and covered the top of the bottle so he could twist out the cork. "You don't have to pretend you were all prepared for something like that. I could tell that using the pie was a last-minute inspiration, just

like my deal with the hammock was totally unplanned.
I think it's great that you're spontaneous. So am I."

She paused, as if absorbing what he'd said. Then she
cleared her throat. "I'm not as sexually experienced as
you are. I suppose you've figured that out, too."

"Well, that makes you just about perfect." He punc-
tured that with the pop of the cork, then poured the
champagne into the glasses she'd set on the counter,
making sure he didn't spill. "Guys dream about finding a woman who isn't quite as experienced as they are
but is ready to try anything."

"I can't be your dream girl."

That got his attention. He stopped pouring and
looked at her.

"Well, I'm sorry, but I just can't." She looked like a
stubborn little kid.

He sighed and put down the bottle. "Kasey, what's
the deal here? This morning you were ready to ditch
me because I came on too strong. Now I make an off-
hand remark about guys who dream about women like
you, and you jump on me as if I've proposed."

She flushed and looked away. "I know you're not
proposing, but it sounded sort of...definite, that's all."

"It wasn't definite, okay?" But he was sick of her acting like he had cooties. "The thing is, I can't help wondering what you find so objectionable about me that
you have to keep reminding me I'm temporary enter-
tainment. Is it my IQ? Is it that I'm not smart enough for
you?"

"That's not fair."

Instantly he was sorry. She'd probably heard that a
hundred times. "Yeah, you're right. I told you I

thought it was fantastic that you're smart, and then I used it against you." He ran a hand through his hair. "But whenever you push me away, I can't help wondering why. I lost my temper. I apologize."

"Maybe I can explain." She took a deep breath. "Let's go in the living room and I'll light the candles."

"Yeah, let's do that." He hated that the mood was spoiled, but when she'd said, straight out, *I can't be your dream girl,* it had hit him where he lived. He thought she might be his dream girl, and he didn't like hearing her reject the idea so completely.

Moments later they were cuddling on her futon couch with the candles burning, and the mood had already improved. He couldn't stay mad at her for long. Besides, he liked snuggling with her.

He liked it too damn much, as a matter of fact. In a setting like this, he started thinking about how nice it would be to cuddle this way every night, and then go to bed and cuddle some more, and wake up next to each other. He could picture Kasey in that role. But she didn't want him to, for some reason.

She took an afghan that had been folded across the back of the futon and spread it over them to ward off the breeze from the air conditioner. Then she took a sip of her champagne. "It's good."

He touched his glass to hers. "So are you. Very good." He didn't make the toast he'd wanted to make, about many more nights like this. She might take it wrong.

"Sam, I haven't dated a lot, haven't had a bunch of lovers."

That made him very happy, but he tried to sound sympathetic. "Because of being so smart."

"That has a lot to do with it, yes. I, um, used to be sort of a nerd."

"Looking at you now, that's hard to believe."

"It's true. Last summer, my...a friend...helped me with a makeover. We did the hair, the clothes, the makeup—all of it."

He caught her chin in one hand. "So exactly what color are your eyes, really?"

"Gray. Totally uninteresting." Then she must have realized how that could sound to someone whose eyes were also gray. "Not that *your* eyes are boring. I like your eyes a lot. You have little flecks of gold in there, but mine are—"

"Would you take out your contacts so I can see for myself if they're totally uninteresting?" He had a hunch he'd like her better without the blue tint. The more she revealed the authentic Kasey Braddock, the more he liked what he saw. Her personality—part child, part woman—fascinated him.

"If I take out my contacts, I'll be blind as a bat."

"I'll bet you have glasses around here somewhere."

"Glasses!" She stared at him in horror. "As if I'd let you see me in glasses! Talk about blowing the entire image. I think not."

"Is that why you don't want me to get too close? You're hung up on creating an image? Because I don't care about that."

"Are you sure?" She skewered him over the rim of her glass. "Think about when we first met. Would you have been as excited about going out with me if I'd walked up to you wearing glasses, dressed in a shapeless denim jumper and with my hair in a braid?''

He wasn't sure he liked this discussion. ''Maybe not,'' he finally admitted. ''But—''

''See? That's my point.''

''But that look is not you, not your personality. You wouldn't deliberately try to make yourself unattractive.''

''Not deliberately, but that's exactly how I used to dress. Needless to say, I didn't have a lot of offers back then.''

He studied her, trying to picture her the way she'd described. ''I'll bet you looked better than that.''

''I could show you pictures.''

''Anybody can take a bad picture.''

''Sam, face facts. If you'd met me a couple of years ago, you wouldn't have given me a second glance.''

Unfortunately, she was probably right. He'd been attracted by her outward appearance, which made him just like all the other guys. He wasn't proud of that.

But he was nothing if not honest. ''Okay, guilty as charged.'' he said. ''I was hooked the minute I saw you get out of your little red convertible with SO REDY on the vanity plate.''

''I'm not surprised...or even offended.'' She sipped her champagne. ''I work in PR, remember? I understand the emotional impact of images. I just didn't have the nerve to apply the principles to myself until recently.''

He could see where this was going. ''So you want to catch up on all the fun you missed during your shapeless-denim-jumper phase?''

"Is that so wrong?" She held his gaze.

"No, of course not." But it shot the hell out of his dreams. "Now that you've explained the situation, I can't help wondering something. You don't have to answer, but I have a feeling this is important to the discussion. Since your makeover, how many guys have you, uh...been with?"

"You mean, how many have I had sex with?"

He sighed. "Yeah, that's what I mean. And I have no right to ask. That's a very personal—"

"One."

"Me?"

"You. I haven't been ready until now. I had to be mentally prepared to live up to my new image, prepared to take on hot guys instead of the nerds I was used to."

That was good news and bad news—he liked having the distinction of being the first hot guy, especially liked being labeled a hot guy. But she'd implied he would be the first of many. That was very bad news. Her casual-sex period could last for years. After all, his had.

"So that's why I said we were at different stages in our lives right now," she said. "Eventually I'll need to move on."

That thought depressed him, so he drank some more champagne.

"In the meantime, though..." She slipped her hand under the afghan and quickly put his penis on red alert.

"I see your point." He loved what she was doing under that afghan. "*Eventually* is a very vague word."

"But *orgasm* is not."

"Nope. Quite specific." And impending, too. He realized there was a problem with walking around naked. No pockets. Much as he hated to do it, he put a stop to her erotic stroking.

"Bring your champagne," he said, throwing back the afghan and standing. "We need to make an expedition back to where the wild condoms grow."

She laughed. "But I could just—"

"I know. You were about to accomplish exactly that." He grabbed the champagne bottle and motioned her to go ahead of him down the hall. "But I have a hankering to try this the old-fashioned way."

"No pies?" she said over her shoulder. "No whipped cream?"

"That's right." In the dim light of the hallway, he could just make out the inviting sway of her hips and the mouthwatering curve of her butt. He'd like to try doggie style some time, but right now, he had some bonding in mind. "And no contacts," he said as they stepped into the darkened bedroom.

"You're ridiculous." She set her glass on the nightstand. "Want me to light the candles?"

"I'd love you to turn on the lamp, instead."

She pushed the little switch and glanced at him. "Full light and no contacts. Are you trying to demystify me?"

I'm trying to learn who you are so I can somehow hang on to you. But of course he couldn't say that, so he gave her another reason that was almost as valid. "I'd like to watch your eyes when you come. I want to see what color they get for real."

She shook her head and smiled, as if unable to believe he could be so goofy. "Okay, if it means that much to you. But I won't be able to see you very well."

"Unless you put on your glasses."

"I draw the line at glasses. Be right back. These aren't disposable, so I have to take them out in the bathroom."

After she left, he took one more drink of his champagne before setting the bottle and his glass next to hers. He noticed how uncluttered the surfaces were in this room. She didn't have any framed family pictures sitting around. Most women he knew loved doing that. No doubt about it, Kasey was a puzzle, a puzzle he wanted to solve.

Stretching out on the bed, he was in a perfect position for her entrance. She walked in holding her hands out in front of her as if she couldn't see a thing.

Then she groped for the edge of the bed. "Where are you, Sam? I can't find you."

If he hadn't seen the corner of her mouth twitch, he would have believed her act. "I'm right here," he said, holding back a smile. "Keep looking."

"I see something...something *enormous.* There!" She grabbed his erect penis. "Got it!"

"Ah, yes, but do you recognize this large object you've found, my dear?"

"It does feel sort of familiar." She fumbled around some more and cupped his balls in her other hand. "I think all this goes together."

"Good guess."

She fondled him some more, keeping her eyes unfocused. "This part feels like something I've touched before.... Sam, is that you?"

"Yeah, it's me, you faker." Laughing, he rolled her to her back. "And I love the color of your eyes."

"You're just saying that." But she was smiling, as if she liked hearing the compliment. "After all this hoopla, you wouldn't dare say anything different."

"Your eyes are the color of clouds before a rain."

"And dishwater before it drains."

He leaned down and kissed her. "Be quiet. We're going to have sex, now."

"I hope you can find the condoms, because I can't even see the box."

"Leave everything to me."

"All righty, then."

And she did leave everything to him. Maybe she sensed that he had a certain experience in mind, because he'd asked her to leave the light on and take her contacts out. Or maybe she felt sad because she couldn't give him any promises about their future.

She did give him all of herself, though, allowing him to kiss and caress every part of her, to map her body completely in the glow of the bedside lamp. And when he finally put on a condom and thrust deep inside her, she let him see the passion building in her eyes...her beautiful gray eyes.

He knew he was falling for her. No doubt she also realized what was happening to him. If only she'd let go of the agenda she was clinging to so desperately. Then she just might fall for him, too.

SAM STAYED FOR BREAKFAST, even though Kasey warned him she didn't know how to cook. He promised to take care of that situation. Then he set the alarm and roused her out of bed at an ungodly hour so they wouldn't have to rush.

While she showered, he borrowed a razor. He insisted he wouldn't kiss her until he'd shaved because he didn't want to give her whisker burn. Then he joined her in the shower, kissing her on the mouth and after that in places that quickly produced her first climax of the day. She returned the favor, and by the time they finally climbed out of the shower, she was very glad her utilities were included in her rent.

After they dressed, she watched in fascination as he poked through her refrigerator and located eggs and butter. He found a skillet she never used, took his time learning the idiosyncracies of her stove, and finally fried the eggs over-easy, exactly the way she liked them. She made the coffee and managed to burn the toast.

Their division of chores felt dangerously domestic to her. The easy way they puttered around the kitchen together was a little unnerving, and she wondered if he'd comment on it. He didn't.

Sharing breakfast at her tiny table in a corner of her living room seemed way too cozy and comfortable, and she searched for a way to change the mood. She settled on discussing the project he'd hired her for. "You never did fill out that questionnaire I need for your PR campaign," she said.

"No. We got sidetracked." He winked at her and continued munching his toast. No guy had any business looking so appealing at seven-thirty in the morning.

"I could ask you the questions now." If she didn't focus on something else, she was liable to drag him back to the bedroom, and they'd both be late for work.

He took a swallow of coffee. "Shoot."

"What message are you conveying with your business currently?"

He looked blank. "Message? I'm not conveying any message."

"Yes, you are, whether you realize it or not." Right now he was conveying the message that he was available for some more mind-blowing sex.

"Then maybe you can tell me what the message is."

That you're hot. With great difficulty she refocused her thoughts and tried to picture the business card he'd given her yesterday. "What else is on your card besides the company name and your contact info?"

"Professional, courteous service."

"There's your message."

"And it's boring. It's not sexy enough."

Oh, but you make up for it. She wondered how many female customers he had. An ad featuring Sam without his shirt would triple his business in no time. But that wasn't the plan he had in mind.

"So that's what you want?" she said. "A sexy message?"

"Yeah." He gazed across the table at her. "That's why I came to you. You know that Springsteen tune 'Secret Garden'?"

"Uh-huh." It was one of her favorite songs in the whole world. She'd nearly worn out that part of the *Jerry Maguire* soundtrack.

"I want that kind of message to come across."

"The song's about sex."

"I know, and I want to help customers create a secret garden right in their own backyards, where they can...do whatever they want."

"Like have sex?"

He smiled at her. "If they want to."

"But of course you can't come right out and say that."

"No. It has to be implied, like in the Springsteen tune. But if you can think how to do it, I guarantee I'll get more business."

She sipped her coffee and turned the problem over in her mind. "How about using the implications of the Springsteen song? Your new slogan could be *Specializing in Secret Gardens.*"

"You're a genius."

"Borderline."

He laughed. "That's close enough for my purposes. I love the slogan. I'm sure we can do lots of great things with it." He reached across the table and captured her hand. "Now let's talk about us, and my garden. I want you to come to my place again. We'll do it right this time, with a meal, candles, soft music and perhaps another visit to the garden."

Her body hummed in anticipation. "Last time wasn't too shabby."

"I can improve on it." He rubbed his thumb over the back of her hand. "Tonight?"

She should probably put him off. Three nights in a row was beginning to look like a serious commitment. Then she tried to imagine how she'd feel, staying home alone when she could be in his garden, in his arms, having multiple orgasms. "Okay," she said.

His eyes blazed with triumph. "Great. And now I'd better leave before I haul you back to bed." He squeezed her hand and released it before scooting his chair away from the table.

"What can I bring?" She stood and walked with him to the door.

"Yourself."

"No, seriously. I'm no cook, but I can pick up something at the deli."

He paused by the door. "There is one thing, but you might not want to get it."

"Sure I would. Bread? Wine? What?"

"Underwear from Slightly Scandalous."

14

Kasey discovered that strolling into Slightly Scandalous as a potential customer was very different from walking in as a PR professional looking for ways to upgrade the store's image. As a buyer, she looked at the displays in a whole new way. Her tummy jumped with nervousness as she tried to decide if she was woman enough to do this or if she was too chicken.

That emphasized exactly why the store needed an image change. If more women could shop for sexy undies with a degree of comfort, the business would survive, maybe even prosper. If too many women came here feeling as she did right now, sales would continue to slide downhill.

"Hi, Kasey!" Monique, a young salesgirl the owner had hired a month ago, smiled. From her pink-and-blond spiked hair to her multiple piercings, Monique fit the old Slightly Scandalous stereotype. She was nineteen, only a year younger than Kasey, but she made Kasey feel ancient.

"Hey, Monique." Kasey wondered if Monique would take kindly to a slight makeover herself, once the store changed its look. A California native, Monique was a freethinker who didn't mind the risqué nature of the shop, but no doubt she wanted to keep her job and understood that business wasn't what it should be. She'd probably cooperate.

"I'll bet you're here to get some more ideas, huh?"

"Something like that," Kasey said. No changes had been made to the displays or the merchandise pending Kasey's presentation of the proposed makeover. Therefore mannequins still wore peekaboo bras and thongs with no crotch. She wondered if that's what Sam envisioned on her tonight.

"I had an idea," Monique said.

"What's that?" Kasey had always thought Monique was creative, so she was more than willing to listen.

"Once the store has relocated with its new look, for some free publicity, you could do a fashion show for some of the businesswomen's clubs in town."

"With underwear?" Kasey wondered how that would go over at a downtown luncheon meeting.

"Sure. You could do it very tastefully, have the models wearing silk robes, and then they sort of flash the underwear. I mean, not like a flasher, but more sort of seductive. You know—sophisticatedly sexy."

Kasey laughed as she imagined how fun and flirty that could be, exactly the image she was trying to create for the store. "I get it. And I think it would work, too, presented like that. Thanks, Monique. If we do that, I'll make sure you get all the credit for the idea."

"Thanks." Monique flushed with pleasure. "And by the way, you'd make a great model."

Kasey gulped. "Oh, I don't think so."

"You would. You have the body for it. You might not want to, seeing as how you're with this big-deal PR company, but you'd be great. I've had some modeling classes. I could teach you how to walk."

"You could?" Kasey couldn't help thinking of a private runway in a secluded little garden with an audience of one. She wouldn't mind some tips on how to model whatever she bought today, *if* she worked up the nerve to buy it.

"I could definitely teach you. Whenever you want. Anyway, I've bothered you enough. You probably came here to prowl around and make notes, like you did last time. Don't let me stop you."

"Um, okay." If Monique hadn't made assumptions about Kasey's reason for being there this morning, she might have been able to confess the real reason. But now she felt obliged to look professional and busy. Taking her voice-activated recorder out of her briefcase, she started moving around the store.

"The leather thong and bra might be able to stay in the line," she murmured into the recorder. *"But the matching handcuffs need to be moved from the front of the store, perhaps to a special room in back. Ditto the riding crop."* She wondered if Sam was into any of that S and M stuff. She couldn't picture him taking it seriously, but as long as it was all in fun, then maybe...

Shaking herself out of an erotic daydream, she walked to another display. *"Silk teddies are one of the key items in a store of this kind, but the customer we're hoping to attract will not want her nipples to show, or her...other parts."*

Or would she? Maybe under certain circumstances she would. For example, if she were carrying on a high-energy affair with a sexy landscaper, she might want to

flaunt her nipples. The more Kasey saw of this underwear with gaps in strategic places, the more she believed that was precisely what Sam hoped she'd bring
to his private party tonight.

If she recommended eliminating all such items from
the store, they might lose customers who wanted a special thrill connected to their purchase. *"Perhaps the answer is to make a private annex available to those who wish to
shop for these items,"* she dictated into the recorder.
*"Think video store, where the bulk of the offerings are for
general consumption, and a special section in the back is dedicated to adult movies."*

No doubt about it, though, something had to be done
about the store's curb appeal. She'd been there nearly
thirty minutes and not a single customer had arrived.
That might change anytime, though, and if she planned
to buy anything, she'd better make her move. But what
should she get?

Monique would be glad to advise her. Kasey walked
over to the counter where the salesclerk was flipping
through the pages of a magazine. Kasey cleared her
throat. "Monique, I could use some help."

"Yeah?" Monique glanced up, her expression eager.
"Great! I love coming up with ideas about how to pro-
mote stuff. I've been thinking I might like a career in
PR. Maybe I'll take some classes."

"You'd be good at PR." They were back to business
and Kasey almost lost her nerve. Monique was setting
her up as a role model, so how could she ask for advice
on crotchless panties? "I encourage you to give it a
try."

"You know, I think I will. So what do you need help with?"

"Well, I... I, um, it's sort of a...a personal matter."

"Oh!"

"I need to buy some really sexy underwear." Kasey rushed on before she changed her mind. "And I want you to help me pick it out, and...and teach me the runway walk."

SAM DIDN'T HAVE TIME to make a meal for Kasey, so he picked up some Thai food on the way home. He'd decided to dismantle the hammock to make room for his latest purchase—a canvas gazebo with side panels that rolled down for privacy. He was struggling with the gazebo when Colin stuck his head over the alley gate.

"Hey, man!" Colin called. "I saw your truck out front but you didn't answer your doorbell, so I thought you might be out here in your favorite spot. What the hell is that, anyway?"

"It's supposed to be a gazebo, but right now it's a pile of canvas and metal pieces that won't cooperate." He abandoned the mess on his patio and walked over to unlock the gate. "So what's up?"

"Not your gazebo, apparently. Want some help?"

"Smart-ass. Sure."

"Then I'm your guy. I played at a gig where they had one of these contraptions." Colin fished a rubber band out of his pocket and put his long hair in a ponytail—his personal signal that he was getting down to work. "Got beer?"

"Yeah, but you'll have to drink it quick. I have a date."

"Cool. Is it that hot chick you brought to the Cactus Club?" Ignoring the directions sitting on the patio table, Colin started putting together braces.

"Aren't you going to take a passing glance at those directions?" Sam knew the answer, but he wanted to divert Colin away from the subject of Kasey. He'd promised her they'd keep their affair secret.

Fortunately Colin was easy to distract. That was one of his problems. The only thing he'd stayed with consistently was his music, and that was why Sam wanted to give him all the support he could.

Sure enough, Colin took the bait and gave Sam a withering glance. "Have you *ever* known me to use directions?"

"Nope. But there's always a first time."

"No, there isn't. Directions only confuse the issue."

"If you say so. I'll get the beer."

When he returned a few minutes later with a bottle of his brother's favorite imported brew, Colin had made good progress on the gazebo. The kid was so bright when he focused. Then something occurred to him. As a very bright person who seemed to have her act together, Kasey might be able to help guide him to stay focused. But Sam wasn't supposed to be fostering a relationship between Kasey and his brother.

"Pick up that side of the canvas top and we'll lift it over the frame," Colin said.

"How do you know that's it's facing right?"

"I channeled the gazebo maker over in China, dude."

Sam laughed, but sometimes he wondered if Colin was joking or not. The kid was amazing. Having Colin around had given him an appreciation for the workings of the right brain and had taught him to admire creative intelligence, not sneer at it.

Kasey might not find a lot of guys who could do that. He wondered how he could subtly point out to her that he, Sam Ashton, was the one for her. And he didn't feel like waiting around tapping his foot while she had sex with a bunch of other guys, either.

Before long the gazebo was finished and Colin claimed his beer. "You're not having one with me?"

"Nah."

"Gotta stay sharp for your gazebo-mate, huh?" Colin grinned at him. "Are you going to put the patio table in there? That would be classy."

"Uh, maybe." Sam wasn't keen on revealing his plans for the gazebo. They didn't involve putting the patio table in it. "When's the next gig for the Tin Tarantulas?"

Colin pointed the beer bottle at him. "Way to read my mind, bro! I swear you're getting better at ESP every day."

Not really. But he was getting better at changing the subject when he didn't want Colin to continue along a certain line of questioning. "So you have something coming up?"

"We do, and it's a big deal. We're booked into that new place, the Yucca Lounge."

Sam had heard of it, a trendy club in Scottsdale. "Isn't that a much bigger venue?"

"Most definitely. Which is why I need your help, man. I want you to call in all your favors for Saturday night, talk to anybody you know. We have to pack that place to the rafters, and I'm nervous. It's huge."

"You'll pull them in," Sam said. "There was standing room only at the Cactus Club."

"We're talkin' twice the number of seats. Please get the word out to everyone in your Rolodex, okay?"

"Okay." Sam nodded and tried to think of helping his brother instead of mourning the loss of a big chunk of his Saturday night. He and Kasey would have to meet afterward, because he couldn't take her, not if she really wanted to keep their affair quiet.

Colin still looked worried. "Like, can you put pressure on your guys at work?"

"Sure. I'll do that. I'll ask them to bring their friends. Don't worry. It'll be fine."

"I can't leave that to chance. This is the time to dredge up everybody you've ever known in Phoenix, man. Drag out your yearbook and start looking for dudes you knew in high school. Me, I can't do that because we moved and I've lost track of everybody."

"I'll find out who's still in town. I've been meaning to look in the phone book and find out if Jim Winston's still here. If he is, maybe he can help me round up some of the other guys."

"Thanks, bro." Colin clapped him on the back. "And bring your girlfriend, and all her friends, too."

"Uh, we'll see."

Colin peered at him. Then he waved his arm at the gazebo. "You just put up a frickin' gazebo for this chick, and you can't bring her on Saturday night?"

"It's complicated."

"Oh, I get it. It's the same chick from the other night, and she secretly hated our music."

"No, she loved your music. That's not the problem."

"Then it must be that she's hot for me and you don't want to take a chance that she'll jump ship."

Sam grinned. "You are such an egomaniac."

"It's true, huh?" Colin laughed. "Don't worry. I'll tell her you're a better deal. Chicks love the steady income."

"Gee, that makes me feel like such a man. I may not be much, but by God, I have a steady income. How sexy can you get?"

Colin finished his beer and handed the bottle to Sam. Then he glanced at the gazebo. "You tell me, bro." Chuckling, he headed for the back gate.

"Hey, thanks for the help."

"Any time. Just round up all the strays you can find for Saturday, okay?"

"Don't worry. I'll charter a bus if I have to."

"Sounds good." With a wave, Colin left.

AFTER BUYING THE UNDERWEAR and getting a quick runway lesson from Monique in the back room of the store, Kasey made one more stop at a dress boutique and found a wraparound silk dress. The ivory material slid over her skin like cool water and was held together by two small ties. Kasey practiced in the dressing room to make sure she could pull the ties apart in seconds.

The dress exactly matched the underwear she'd bought at Slightly Scandalous. She would have to drive very carefully over to Sam's house. If she got into an accident and was taken to the E.R. in this outfit, her mother would never forgive her.

She stowed her loot in the trunk of her Miata before returning to the office. Gretchen and the gang were already convinced she was keeping secrets about Sam. They didn't need to find a shopping bag from Slightly Scandalous to make them even more suspicious.

She spent the rest of the morning on the lingerie store's new image, and the afternoon dreaming up promo ideas for Ashton Landscaping. Sam's enthusiasm for her ideas felt good. Everything about Sam felt good. If she were looking for the perfect guy, Sam would be it.

But she was only twenty years old. She wasn't ready for the perfect guy. Life was so unfair. Now that she was ready to experience being a swinging single girl, she was supposed to find men who were fun, not perfect. She'd read the chick-lit books—nobody found Mr. Perfect right off the bat. Except her, apparently.

Maybe Sam wasn't as right for her as he seemed. She wasn't very experienced, so she might not recognize his imperfections. The fact that she considered him perfect should be a warning bell in itself. He was human— there had to be things wrong with him.

Maybe tonight she'd try to be more objective and figure out where Sam was lacking. It wouldn't be in the area of sex, so she could simply enjoy that part and look for flaws in other parts of his life. And she *would* enjoy the sex. She could hardly wait to show off her Bad Girl duds.

At last the day crawled to an end. She hurried home, showered and changed into her outfit. As she headed out the door, she picked up the folder containing her plans for his promo campaign. Because they'd agreed he wouldn't come into the office, she had to discuss business sometime during the night.

She was surprised at how natural that seemed, mixing their private and professional lives. Apparently he'd known what he was talking about when he'd insisted she could do his PR work even though they were having a hot and heavy affair.

The situation could change, though, if the affair ended before the promo campaign. They might not work together so easily if one of them decided to call off the fireworks. And someone would do that sooner or later.

But she refused to think about that now, while she was wearing underwear from Slightly Scandalous and contemplating Sam's reaction. She smiled as she turned into the driveway of Sam's cute little house. Tonight would be another outstanding night of sex. She should have brought champagne.

15

SAM BARELY MADE IT through all the preparations, but when the doorbell rang, he'd finished everything. Candles in glass containers ringed the patio and sat on the table, which was set for two. Exotic music drifted from his portable CD player.

He'd covered the floor of the gazebo with an egg-crate mattress topper plus quilts and pillows. Three sides were rolled down, but he'd left the fourth side up, so that Kasey could see what he had in mind for after dinner. He wanted to create some anticipation in her, too.

When he opened the door and saw her standing there in an ivory silk dress that looked like it would come off in no time, he wanted to forget about anticipation, forget about dinner completely, in fact. "Hi," he said. "I see you brought dessert."

"You think so?" She smiled and moved past him.

"Yeah, and it smells delicious." He loved dealing with a smart woman, someone who didn't have to ask what he meant by bringing dessert.

She turned and held out a folder. "I have more ideas for your promo plan, if you want to hear them."

"I do." He took the folder and put it on the coffee table. "Later. Much, much later." Then he slid his arm around her waist. Silk was so touchable, especially when it was wrapped around Kasey. "Right now, I want you to come with me. By the way, thanks for wearing your clear contacts tonight."

"Anything for you, Sam."

"Good to know." He wished he could take her statement literally, but he knew there were limits to what she'd do for him. Making a long-term commitment was out of the question, for example, at least for now. He had to stop thinking about that and focus on the present.

Fortunately, when he opened the kitchen door and guided her outside, her response to his efforts was exactly what he'd hoped. She laughed with delight.

"Like it?"

"I *love* it. Arabian Nights, here we come. But I forgot my seven veils."

"You won't need seven veils to get my attention." He leaned down and stole a quick kiss. One made him want more, but he forced himself to release her while they still had some control over themselves. "Have a seat at the table. I'll bring out the food."

"Can I do anything to help?"

He raked her silk dress with a glance. "If you follow me into the kitchen we'll end up having sex on the floor."

"Is that a bad thing?"

"Depends on how much you like cold lemongrass soup and spoiled chicken with peanut sauce."

Her eyes widened. "Wow. Sounds as if you went to a whole lot of trouble."

"No, the restaurant did."

She looked at him with affection in her gray eyes.

"Even so, I'm impressed with all you've done, and I don't want to ruin your careful setup. I'll stay out here and let you serve the food."

"Okay. I'll be right back." He was dying to know what she was wearing under that dress and whether she'd accepted his challenge to pay a visit to Slightly Scandalous today. But anticipation would make the discovery that much sweeter. Even without audacious underwear she would be a joy to undress, as usual.

Moments later he returned carrying a tray loaded with the first course. But instead of walking straight over to the table, he paused to take in the scene. Kasey was facing away from him as she sat quietly, her attention on the candle flame in front of her. Her shining blond hair hung straight down, looking as silky and touchable as her dress. Although the dress was simply styled, the color reminded him of weddings, and he was hit with a longing that was as fierce as it was sudden.

In that moment he knew that everything he wanted was right here. If he could have Kasey, a couple of kids, a little house, a quiet garden and a decent job, he'd be a happy man. But if he told her that, she'd leave and never come back.

He cleared a lump from his throat. "Dinner is served," he said, and she turned to smile at him. Oh, yeah, she was everything he wanted and more. It might take a miracle for them to be together, but he wasn't giving up, not yet.

As they ate their spicy meal in the glow of candle-light, Kasey worked hard to come up with drawbacks to Sam Ashton. She wasn't having much luck. He was generous, sexy, hardworking and eager to please her.

Yes, he'd admitted that a woman's looks affected his judgment. So, that simply meant he wasn't any different from the majority of men on the planet. She thought it might be a function of the male mind-set, handed down from the caveman days.

Basically the only problem with Sam was his age. Even that was an asset right now, because his greater experience encouraged her to be sexually courageous. And he liked that she was smart. That was a refreshing change. She didn't have to hide her brains from Sam.

Oh, why did she have to meet Sam now? Why couldn't she have met him five years from now? But she knew the answer to that. Five years from now Sam would be married...to someone else. She hated that idea.

While they ate, Sam told her about Oregon, a place she'd never seen. He didn't suggest taking her there to see it, and she knew why. She'd made her rules very clear, and he was doing his best to abide by them.

Maybe he expected to change her mind about those rules with this elaborate effort tonight. If that was his intent, he was doing a damned good job. Sitting here drinking wine with Sam while music provided a sensuous background was the kind of romantic setting she'd often fantasized about. Maybe she'd be a fool to throw it all away so that she could have a series of unsatisfying sexual episodes.

She had to assume that sex with other guys would be unsatisfying. Sam had set the bar pretty damned high.

After being with him, she couldn't imagine how any other man would measure up.

He set down his wineglass, stood and held out his hand. "Dance with me."

"Sure." And when she left the table and moved into his arms, the old cliché came true—they did seem to be two halves creating a whole. They moved together across the uneven flagstone as if the surface were glass.

He held her lightly, as if he didn't need to press her against his body to let her know how much he wanted her. The message was in his eyes and the tender way he circled her palm with his thumb. He seemed content to wait, knowing they'd soon be locked in passion, writhing sensuously on the quilts he'd laid down inside the gazebo.

He didn't speak, but his expression told her more than words what he was feeling. He wouldn't say it out loud, because she'd warned him not to tie her down. As they danced under the desert moon, she wondered what was so bad about being tied down to a guy as wonderful as Sam. She hadn't wanted to fall in love with him, but it was happening, anyway.

SAM COULD SEE the resistance melting in Kasey's eyes. Every second that passed, she was less afraid of her feelings, more willing to believe in her instincts. He allowed himself to hope, just a little.

Unimportant as it might seem to her, looking into her eyes while she wore clear contacts made a huge difference. He no longer had the impression she was putting up a barrier between them. She might be giving him a glimpse of the real Kasey, and that was very encouraging. When a woman did that, she was learning to trust.

Desire teased him, arousing him in lazy increments, becoming gradually more insistent. At last the slow dancing wasn't enough to satisfy the ache building inside him.

He tightened his grip on her waist. "I want you," he murmured. It was all he was allowed to say. It would have to do.

She ran her tongue over her lips. "I want you, too."

What he'd give for her to change the four-letter word in that sentence. But the night was young. His heart beat faster as he thought of what was ahead. "Then maybe it's time for the sheikh to take the maiden into his tent and ravish her."

"Or maybe it's time for the sheikh to wait in his tent and let the maiden come to him."

"Oh?" A shiver of excitement shot up his spine. "I thought you forgot your seven veils."

"There are other ways for a maiden to please her sheikh."

"And will I be pleased?" He had an idea that Slightly Scandalous had something to do with this. Hot damn.

"Yes, I believe you will be very pleased." She stepped out of his arms. "Go into the tent and wait for my entrance."

"An entrance, huh? This is sounding better and better." He walked over to the gazebo and took off his shoes before ducking under the canopy.

If she'd bought sexy underwear because he'd asked her to, that was an excellent sign. Then again, maybe he was still serving as her testing ground. That was such a depressing thought that he shoved it back into the pit where his other insecurities lived and slammed the lid shut.

He sat down on the cushy surface and glanced outside. She was gone. She hadn't been kidding about making an entrance. His pulse rate jumped several more beats per minute. He was probably supposed to play the bored potentate. He lounged back against a large floor pillow but kept his head propped on one hand so he didn't miss anything.

Then he saw her, poised about five yards away, her chin lifted, her feet bare. Her gaze locked with his as she started toward him, striding exactly as he'd seen fashion models walk. He wondered where she'd learned that. Then his brain went on overload as she slowly untied her dress.

Once the tie was free, the dress didn't fall open as he'd hoped. Apparently there was a second tie inside. Kasey paused and drew back the part of the dress that was loose, and he nearly swallowed his tongue. The ivory bra she wore was one of the cutout affairs. He caught a glimpse of one rosy nipple before she closed the lapel, holding it lightly against her body as she continued toward him.

Fascinated and incredibly aroused, he watched her slip her hand under the shimmering silk to unfasten the second tie. Then she paused again and slowly drew aside the silk.

He forgot to breathe.

The view was more spectacular than he could have imagined in a hundred years of sexual daydreams. Her breasts thrust boldly through the openings in the ivory bra, but he'd been expecting that after the first teasing peek. He hadn't dared to expect the rest—a thong designed not to cover, but to set off and highlight that blond triangle where he would gladly lose himself for hours.

Then she drew her dress closed again, removing the visual treat she'd allowed him for a fleeting moment. He moaned in protest. She smiled and gave him another quick flash before pulling the silk back in place.

Then she turned and began walking away.

"*No.*" His voice came out as an embarrassing croak.

She continued to walk, and he sat up, prepared to go after her. But before he got to his feet, he realized that she was letting the dress slide off her shoulders. He sank back to the quilt, his mouth going dry. The dress dangled from her arms, and in the flickering candlelight, he had an erection-producing view of her sleek backside as she moved steadily away from him. Nothing touched her there except the thin strap of the thong. He wanted to be that strap.

She stopped, tossed back her hair and glanced over her bare shoulder at him. He would take that image to his grave. As his heart threatened to jump clear out of his chest, she let the dress slip off completely, although she caught it before it hit the flagstone. She stayed that way, her back to him, for what seemed like an eternity.

Finally, with a flick of her wrist, she tossed the dress over her shoulder and turned to face him, giving him a full frontal view of that bodacious outfit. Like a jungle cat on the prowl, she sauntered boldly toward the gazebo. He wondered if he'd embarrass himself by having a climax before she arrived.

She walked straight into the tent and right over to where he sat. Standing with legs braced wide, she looked down at him. "Well, what do you think?"

He made some incoherent sound deep in his throat. Swallowing, he tried again. "Closer."

"Me?"

"You."

And when she complied, he cupped that delicious behind of hers and did what any man worth his salt would do when presented with crotchless underwear. He enjoyed his dessert.

From the way she moaned and clutched his head, she enjoyed serving it up for him nearly as much as he savored the fare. She began to shake, and he held her tighter, supporting her with both hands as she rushed toward her climax. How he managed to give her one without exploding himself was a true marvel.

Somehow he held off until her shudders eased, but she was still quaking in the aftermath when he urged her down to the quilt. In seconds he'd unzipped and grabbed a condom from the stash in a corner of the gazebo. He didn't take time to do more than open his fly and wrench down his briefs—the urgency was too great.

Then he was thrusting, stroking, pumping frantically, needing to bury himself deep while she still wore that crazy thong. A woman with no underwear was wild enough, but a woman with underwear built specifically for sex—that was the ultimate turn-on.

He felt her tighten and slowed a fraction to allow her to catch up. Braced on his outstretched arms, he blinked the sweat from his eyes so that he wouldn't miss the sight of her breasts, captured in satin yet brazenly exposed to her lover. He leaned down and tugged on her nipple with his teeth.

That must have put her over the edge, because with a gasping cry, she climaxed again. When her contractions began to roll over his hot penis, he thrust one last time and came in a delirious rush of pleasure. As his world spun out of control, he cried out in gratitude.

Long moments later, he'd recovered enough to shuck his clothes so he could cuddle with her skin-to-skin in a tangle of quilts. In that moment, he couldn't imagine how she'd think they would ever call it quits. With this performance it almost seemed as if she'd intended to make him her slave for life. If so, she'd succeeded beyond her wildest dreams.

KASEY FELT OUTRAGEOUSLY PROUD of herself. Talk about being a Bad Girl—she was a certified member of the club now. Poor Sam, he'd been a puppet on a string once she'd started untying her dress. She smoothed his hair as he lay beside her, his head pillowed on her breast.

The way he'd reacted had been adorable. But then, she'd known he would love whatever she tried to do. He was that kind of guy—appreciative. Fun to be with. *Easy to love.*

Oh, boy. There was the problem. Sam wasn't the sort to disappoint a girl, and he'd been doing a fantastic job of making her happy ever since they'd met. How was she supposed to keep from falling in love, when he insisted on being so terrific?

"You did it." His voice was rich with satisfaction. "You went there and bought this stuff. For me."

"Well, I got a little something out of the experience, myself."

"I hope so." He propped his head on his hand. "How does it feel, wearing something like this?"

"Kinky. It's not the most comfortable underwear I've ever owned, and I couldn't stand it for a whole day, but for a few hours, it sure encourages you to think about sex all the time."

"If I'd known you had this on, we wouldn't have made it through dinner." He stroked the exposed part of her breast. "In fact, I probably would have ripped the ties of that dress so I could get to what was underneath."

"I thought I might rip them, too, because I was shaking so much."

"You were? I couldn't tell. You looked like you had it all together."

She smiled. "That's what you were supposed to think. Anyway, on the off chance I'd rip the dress, I brought a change of clothes and left them in the car."

His expression brightened. "Does that mean you can leave for work from here in the morning?"

"No, not really." She noticed as the light left his eyes. He might not disappoint her, but she always seemed to be disappointing him. "I didn't bring makeup or my briefcase." She'd made that decision consciously, though. Coming prepared to spend the night and go directly to work from his place sent a certain message. Next he'd suggest she move a few things into his closet, and then—

"I didn't mean to push."

"I know."

"Forget I said that." He continued to toy with her breasts. Finally he leaned over and began running his tongue around her nipples.

Her worry about their situation eased with every swipe of his tongue. Sex didn't solve anything, but it pushed the problems away for a while. And she wanted him again. She couldn't believe how quickly her desire returned, even after she'd been so completely satisfied a moment ago.

"Keep that up and I'll forget my own name," she said.

His answering chuckle told her he was ready to change the subject back to sex, too. He raked her nipple with his teeth while he ran his hands over the bits of satin outlining her breasts. "I suppose you want to take this off, now."

"Not necessarily." Not while she was watching him caress her through the openings in the bra. It was quite a turn-on.

"How about this?" He ran his finger around the crotchless thong.

"Do you want me to leave it?"

"Uh-huh." He stroked his palm down over her damp curls and slid two fingers inside her slick heat. "It's like an open invitation. I'd never get tired of seeing you in this."

"Sure you would." Although when he rubbed his fingers back and forth, she wasn't sure of anything except that another orgasm was on the way.

"No. I wouldn't. And I do believe I'm going to accept that open invitation one more time."

"Good."

"Yes, it will be." He rolled away long enough to get another condom. Then he was back, moving between her legs, not so frantic as he had been earlier. And when he pushed deep, he held her gaze. "I'll only say this once, but I hope you'll think about it."

"Sam, I—"

"This sort of happiness doesn't come along every day."

She swallowed. "I know. But—"

"Never mind, Kasey. Never mind anything. Just come for me."

And very quickly, she did. He kissed her while she climaxed, muting her cries of release so they wouldn't alarm his neighbors too much. Then he followed soon after, muffling his groans of completion against her shoulder.

And as they lay together, holding each other close, she knew he was right. Happiness was within her grasp. If she let it slip away, there was no guarantee she'd ever find it again.

16

SAM ACCEPTED the idea that he had to be patient with Kasey. They spent the night making love, sleeping a little, discussing his promo campaign, finishing the last of the wine, eating ice cream he'd forgotten he had in the back of his freezer. With each passing hour, he believed he was making progress. She'd look at him for long moments at a time, and he could almost hear her thinking. That was good.

She was a smart woman, and smart women didn't make stupid mistakes—like giving up the best relationship they'd ever had. He certainly wouldn't make that mistake, but it wasn't all up to him. And he'd had more experience in this and knew how rare their interaction was.

Ever the optimist, he hoped she'd say something definitive before she left in the gray light of dawn. She'd changed into her spare outfit, shorts and a T-shirt, and she stood with him by the front door as they exchanged a few more sleepy kisses.

"You're sure you're okay to drive?" he asked.

"I'm fine to drive." She kissed him again. "We got some rest."

"Not much. But I'm not complaining." He couldn't worry about a little sleep when his whole future was on the line. "So what about tonight?"

"Let's see—it's Friday, right?"

He had to stop and figure it out. "Yes. Friday. Do you want to go somewhere? A movie?" If she said yes, then maybe she was giving up on the secrecy. He would be happy to give that up. They wouldn't flaunt their relationship around her office, but he didn't think anyone would have a problem with it, anyway.

She frowned as if turning the idea over in her head. "We could go away for the weekend," she said at last. "Not anywhere that costs a lot, but up in the mountains they have some—"

"I can't this weekend." And he sincerely regretted that. A whole weekend together might really change her mind about their relationship. But he'd promised Colin.

"Oh. Well, then—"

"Colin has another gig Saturday night. Do you want to go?"

He prayed she'd say yes, that she'd love to go. That would solve everything. They'd go hear the Tin Tarantulas and let everyone know they were together. But he didn't want to push the idea and risk scaring her away.

"Let me think about it," she said.

"Okay." He tried not to let his disappointment show.

He must have failed, because she slid her arms around his neck and stood on tiptoe to kiss him. "I'm confused right now, Sam," she murmured. "I thought I knew exactly how I wanted things to be, but now I'm not sure. I've been thinking about what you said. I really have."

"That's all I ask. Take your time."

"Let's go for a drive tonight, away from the city. We can sit and talk."

He wasn't above playing his trump card. He nuzzled her neck and cupped her breast. "And make out a little in the back seat of my car?"

She wiggled closer. "I could probably be persuaded."

"Then wear something that's easy to get off."

"Shall we say seven?"

He didn't want to wait that long. "Shall we say six-thirty?"

She laughed and kissed him full on the mouth. Then she released him. "Six. And this time I'll skip the underwear completely. How's that?"

"Lady, you don't even have to ask. Are you sure you have to leave right this minute?"

"Yes." She opened the door and blew him a kiss. "Six o'clock."

"I'll be there with condoms on."

She grinned at him. "Bye, Sam."

"Bye, Kasey." After the door closed, he stood there awhile and wished he didn't feel so damned unsure about where they were headed. He fought the urge to go after her and demand that she be completely honest about what she felt. Surely she'd have to admit that she was falling in love with him. She'd have to or risk lying. He'd seen love in her eyes thirty seconds ago.

Then he heard the sound of her little red convertible pulling out of his driveway. He'd lost the chance to force her to say something, and no doubt that was for the best. Thinking about her car brought up the memory of when he'd first seen her and noticed her vanity plate—SO REDY.

He'd thought it was a brazen invitation from a woman ready for adventure, sexual or otherwise. Now he realized it was a brave attempt to become something she'd never been. In some ways, like with the Slightly Scandalous underwear, she'd started living up to that plate. But in other ways, she was still afraid—afraid to trust herself to make the right decision.

After all, they'd only known each other a few days. He needed to cut her some slack, give her more time. Eventually, she'd come around to his way of thinking. He smiled. *Eventually*. Such a vague word. *Orgasm*. Such a definite word. He'd concentrate on orgasms, and let *eventually* take care of itself.

BY ALL RIGHTS, Kasey knew she should be tired. Instead she was a mass of worries and wouldn't have been able to sleep even if she'd had the time. She loved Sam and wanted to be with him. She no longer cared about all the other guys she was supposed to get Bad Girl experience from.

And yet she was only twenty. How could she commit to Sam at such a young age? Her parents and Jim would probably hate the idea, although maybe not after they got to know Sam again. They'd liked him once upon a time, when he'd been Jim's buddy.

And that was the other thing—she was very afraid of how Sam would react if he found out how young she was. He'd fallen for a woman he thought was close to his age. Knowing the truth about her could change everything, but if she was seriously considering giving in to her emotions regarding Sam, then she'd have to tell him.

She needed advice, but she couldn't go to her friends in the office. Sam was a client, and the client issue was weird enough without bringing the whole office in on their love affair. Even more important, everyone in the office thought she was older, just as Sam did. They wouldn't understand the scope of the problem unless she revealed her age, which she wasn't about to do.

Only one person might be able to help, and Kasey hesitated to call her. Alicia and Jim had broken up several months ago, and Kasey had a bad feeling that she'd been part of the reason. Jim hadn't been happy with Kasey's makeover. A typical big brother, he was much more comfortable when she wore glasses and denim jumpers.

But after thinking about the problem for most of the morning and getting very little done at work, Kasey decided to risk calling Alicia. She asked if Alicia would consider meeting her for lunch.

"I would love to do that!" Alicia said. "I've missed you!"

"This isn't about Jim," Kasey said quickly, afraid Alicia might misunderstand the call.

"That's okay. In fact, I was sad when we lost touch after Jim and I broke up. It doesn't seem fair that I should lose you as a friend, too."

"You're right. And the fact is, I desperately need some advice."

Alicia laughed. "According to Jim, I'm the worst person to give you advice."

"I don't see it that way. Can we meet at noon at the

Coco's down the road from my office? That's about halfway between your work and mine."

"I'll be there."

"Great. See you then." Kasey hung up feeling much better. Alicia would help her figure this out.

AS KASEY WALKED into the restaurant, she found Alicia at once. She'd cut her dark hair short, but otherwise she looked the way Kasey remembered her—tall and vivacious, with strong features and a ready smile. Kasey thought Jim had holes in his head for breaking up with her.

"You look fabulous," Alicia said when they'd settled into a booth. "Are the guys swarming around or what?"

"Well, one particular one is, but I haven't told him I'm only twenty."

"Ah. Afraid he'll freak?"

"Partly. Here's the weird part. I knew him twelve years ago, when he was in Jim's senior class."

Alicia's carefully made-up eyes widened. "And he doesn't know that, either, I'll bet. Or remember you. And of course you have a different last name from Jim."

"Exactly. So I thought I'd just have some fun and then walk away. I had a crush on him twelve years ago, so it was—"

"Too tempting to resist."

"Right."

The waitress arrived and Alicia chose something quickly, as if not really interested in the food. Kasey picked the same menu item as Alicia to save time.

After the waitress left to fill their order, Alicia turned back to Kasey. "I completely understand why you'd go for him, even knowing the age difference."

Kasey sighed with relief. She'd made the right decision, calling Alicia. "The thing is, Sam's really a great guy. Everything between us is...wonderful. He's pushing for some kind of commitment, and to be honest, I'm falling for him, too. But I'm only twenty."

Alicia smiled. "You don't look it."

"Thanks to you, I don't. And Sam has no idea. I'm sure he thinks I'm at least twenty-five, maybe older. I told him that until recently I'd looked like such a nerd that I hadn't had many dates, and that now I want to find out what it's like to be single and attractive."

"I'll bet that went over like a lead balloon."

Kasey thought about Sam's struggle to understand her position. "He's trying to see it my way. But I'm not being fair to him. Plus, I'm beginning to wonder if I'd be stupid to break up with him so I could date a lot of other guys who wouldn't be nearly as great as Sam."

Alicia leaned forward. "Kasey, you have to tell him how old you are. Then see how he reacts. Right now he doesn't have enough information about you. He's falling for someone he doesn't really know."

What a depressing thought. But Kasey knew Alicia was right. The fantasy had been terrific, but she had to level with Sam and take a chance he'd dump her...or he wouldn't. "Let's say he doesn't run screaming into the night when he finds out I'm twenty and the kid sister of one of his high-school friends. Let's say he doesn't feel horribly betrayed because I misled him. Let's say he gets over both of those hurdles and still wants me. Am I crazy to consider tying myself down?''

Alicia studied her for several seconds. "Have you imagined your life without him?"

"Yes."

"And how does that seem to you?"

"Horrible. Sad. A complete waste."

"Then there's your answer, Kase. We don't always get to have things turn out the way we planned."

Kasey looked across the table at the woman she'd hoped would become her sister-in-law. "I know. It was mostly my fault that you broke up with Jim, wasn't it?"

"No, no, no." Alicia reached over, grabbed Kasey's hand and squeezed it. "Don't go on that guilt trip, Kase. If it hadn't been you, it would have been some other situation where I acted independently and disagreed with his take on things. But here's the punch line—I think he's having a change of heart."

"Jim?" Kasey sat up straighter. "When did this happen?"

"This morning. He called right after I talked to you. Talk about weird karma."

Kasey gasped. "You didn't tell him you were meeting me, did you? Because I don't want him asking questions until—"

"Sweetie, of course not. What's between you and me is private. But Jim asked if I'd go out with him Saturday night. It seems a friend of his called, and his little brother is playing in a band... Kasey, what on earth is wrong? You look positively green."

Her stomach pitched. This couldn't be happening.

"Sam is the friend who called him. Sam's little brother has a band."

"Well, that *is* a coincidence. But it doesn't have to mean anything, does it? I mean, just because your Sam called Jim, that doesn't mean that they talked about you."

"Maybe not." Kasey tried to calm down, but she had a bad feeling about the whole thing. "It's just that Sam hasn't contacted Jim since he came back to town. If they talked on the phone this morning, Jim might have decided to fill Sam in on the family, tell him what everybody's up to."

"Or not."

"Or not. But I'd hate for Sam to find out who I am by accident from someone else. The truth is, I *did* mislead him, and I want to be the one who tells him so." They'd been dating only a few days, and she'd kidded herself that she had plenty of time to confess. She might already be too late.

"Of course you want to tell him yourself, and I'll bet you'll be able to tonight."

"I'll have to make it tonight. Jim will be seeing him tomorrow night."

"And will you be going to hear the band?"

Kasey looked across the table at Alicia. "I don't know yet. Listen, would you excuse me for a minute so I can make a quick call?"

"No problem. I'll check my messages, too." Alicia pulled out her cell phone.

Kasey did the same, located Sam's card and punched in his mobile number. When he didn't pick up, she left a message to have him call her. She needed to hear his voice before they met tonight. If he sounded completely normal, then he hadn't discussed her with Jim.

Sam didn't return the call during lunch. Kasey forced herself to concentrate on Alicia, who seemed thrilled that Jim was back in touch.

"He said he's had time to do a lot of thinking, and he was wrong to try and control me," Alicia said. "He's a good guy. He just had some growing up to do. Now maybe he's old enough for me." She laughed.

Kasey smiled, happy for Alicia even though worry about Sam was eating at her gut. Maybe age wasn't as important as she'd thought. Alicia and Jim were exactly the same numerical age but hadn't been the same mental age according to Alicia. Kasey had always been old for her years, so she and Sam might be exactly right. It felt that way.

Now if only he would call her.

BUT SAM DIDN'T CALL. Kasey tried every number she had for him, and he was always unavailable. The sick feeling in the pit of her stomach wouldn't go away. She told herself not to buy trouble, but by the time she drove home to get ready for their date, she was convinced that Sam knew the truth, and that was why he was avoiding her. Nobody liked finding out that a person they'd trusted had been deliberately hiding information about themselves, and hearing it from a third party was the worst way to get the news.

As she packed a small knapsack of munchies for the drive, she tried to think what she'd do if he failed to show up tonight. Finally she decided that if he hadn't arrived by six-thirty, she'd go to his house. If necessary,

she'd scale the wall around his patio and wait for him
there. He'd have to come home some time, and she'd
make him listen. But maybe she wouldn't have to do
any of that, because maybe Sam would arrive as scheduled and then she'd have the whole evening to work
up to her confession.

A good round of sex in the back seat of his car might
make that confession easier. She'd had him wound
around her little finger the night before when she'd
flashed him with her crotchless panties. If she picked
just the right moment to give him the news, he might
be fine with it. She was probably stressing over nothing. He might even laugh and tell her she was silly to
worry about such a small matter.

Nevertheless, she constantly checked through her
living-room window to see if she spied his car pulling
into the parking lot. When it did, at two minutes before
six, she sighed in relief. Crawling over a patio wall
seemed too much like stalking and it wasn't really her
style.

Maybe Sam had been busy all day—simple as that.
The important thing was that he'd shown up when
they'd agreed upon. She'd done her part, wearing elas-
tic-waist shorts, a T-shirt and no underwear whatso-
ever. If that wasn't cooperation, she didn't know what
was.

When Sam rang the doorbell, her heart started
pounding. Well, so she was a little bit nervous. Sometime before the night was out she had to tell him the
very small details she'd left out. Surely they wouldn't
matter too much, and he'd forgive her for the slight de-
ception. She could explain it all in such a way that he'd

understand perfectly. And then they'd have some more sex.

She opened the door with a smile. Her smile vanished the moment she saw his face.

"What in *hell* were you thinking?"

As she absorbed the fury in his eyes, she knew this was going to be bad. Very, very bad.

17

SAM HELD TIGHT to his anger, ignoring a rush of sympathy for Kasey. She looked devastated, but he couldn't weaken toward her now. He walked into the room and slammed the door, for emphasis. She flinched. Too bad. She'd lied to him, and that hurt. A lot.

"Sam, I can explain. I—"

"I thought you had a little problem because you'd just gotten over a nerdy phase and wanted to spread your wings!" He glared at her. "I thought you might be younger than me, maybe by several years, but I never dreamed you were only *twenty*. You're just a baby!"

"I am not!" Her chin came up in defiance, but there were tears gathering in her eyes.

"Oh, yes, you are." He tried to block his awareness of the outfit she'd worn, an outfit he'd specified for back-seat sex. "I remember being twenty, and I didn't know shit from shinola back then." He turned away from her, unable to continue looking at the woman he still wanted and couldn't have. "Little Kasey Winston. And I sent you off to buy crotchless underwear."

"Don't call me that!"

He glanced back at her. "It's who you are, although I never would have recognized you. I guess I know where you got that little scar on your lip, don't I? Oh, and by the way, I didn't tell Jim anything about us. That's partly so he won't lecture you, but mostly so he won't beat the crap out of me."

"I wouldn't let him do that." Her voice shook. "Sam, you don't understand. Please let me explain."

"I probably do understand—at least some of it. Jim told me you charged right through school and had your Bachelor's by the time you were eighteen. He said you were trying to pass as someone older, especially at work, and I get that. But why in hell's name did you have to deceive me, of all people?" Damned if he didn't have a lump in his throat. He swallowed hard, trying to get rid of it.

She looked as if he'd propped her in front of a firing squad. She was obviously scared but determined to take what was coming to her. "You might as well know everything. All the women in the office watched you from the window. Then we drew straws to see who would ask you out. I got the long straw."

He'd thought he couldn't feel worse, but he'd been wrong. His throat hurt, and his voice rasped harshly. "You did it on a dare?"

"Sort of."

"Did you know it was me?"

"Yes."

"Oh, Kasey." He walked over and stared sightlessly out her living-room window. "So you knew all along that nothing could come of this, and yet you still..." He shook his head, unable to go on.

"I didn't...didn't mean for anyone to g-get hurt."

He didn't need to turn around to know she was crying. He felt like crying, too. "Well, I did get hurt. And at some point you had to know that was liable to happen. Damn it, Kasey, you as good as lied to me." He braced his hand against the wall and lowered his head, fighting for control. He wanted to go over there and comfort her, but he couldn't let himself do that. He hated hearing her cry. Worse yet, he still wanted her.

She choked back a sob. "You're right. I lied and I knew you could get hurt. There's really no excuse for that. I meant to end things that first night, but then I started to care for you, too. And I began to think that maybe it could work, after all. I was going to say that tonight, plus tell you how old I was."

"You thought maybe it could work?" He spun around, unable to believe she'd said such a thing. "I don't care how young you are, you should be old enough to know better than that. How could you think for one second I'd expect a twenty-year-old woman to give up all that precious time of exploring, finding herself—hell, *growing up?* Never in a million years would I ask that of you."

"But what if I don't want to—"

"You don't know what you want."

"Yes, I do!"

"Come on, Kasey. Two days ago you were saying you couldn't commit to me because you'd been a nerd and wanted to be a glam girl on the loose for a while."

She took a ragged breath. "So I've changed my mind."

"But there's one thing you can't change, and that's your age. If only you'd told me the truth that first night. If only you'd said *Sam, I'm twenty years old.* The commitment discussion would have been *over,* Kasey."

"And we...we would have been over, too."

"Yes, we damn sure would have. I'm way too attracted to you, and my days of casual sex are gone."

"Don't you see? So are mine! I love you, Sam!"

He winced. How he'd longed to hear her say that. And now she had. But he couldn't trust her to know her own mind. He sighed. "I know you think you do, but—"

"I do!" She hurled herself into his arms. "I didn't want to love you, but I can't help it." Tears streamed from her eyes. "And I think I just lost one of my contacts and my nose is running and I need—"

"You need me out of your life." Gently he set her away from him. It was the toughest thing he'd ever done. "And you may not believe this, but I'm leaving because I happen to love you, too."

"Oh, spare me!" She swiped at her eyes. "Please don't tell me you're doing this for my own good!"

"Okay, I won't tell you that." He reached for the doorknob. "But it's the truth. Goodbye, Kasey." He went out the door and closed it behind him. As he walked away, he heard a thump, as if some object had hit the door. She'd thrown something. Well, after all, she was only twenty.

KASEY CRIED until her eyes hurt and her throat was raw. But gradually the tears dried up, and she was left lying on the carpet, staring at the door. She'd grabbed the closest thing to throw, which had turned out to be the little knapsack of goodies she'd packed for their drive out of town. Fortunately nothing in the canvas bag was breakable.

After getting to her hands and knees, she crawled to the bag, sat down and opened it. She'd put a package of Pepperidge Farm cookies in there, the kind with chocolate filling. She grabbed the package, broke the seal and took out a cookie. Cookies might make her think better, and she had some serious thinking to do.

According to all her test scores, she was nearly a genius. And if a woman who was nearly a genius, even if she happened to be only twenty years old, couldn't solve this problem and get Sam back, then what good were brains, anyway? So she would solve this problem, because she had to get Sam back. The minute he'd walked out the door, she'd finally known for certain that he was her forever-after man.

She also believed with all her heart that she was his forever-after woman. So by bringing them back together, she'd be doing both of them a tremendous favor. She smiled softly. Once she accomplished that she'd try not to remind him of it too often. Maybe just once a year, on their wedding anniversary. And they *would* have a wedding anniversary, because sometime in the next year they would have a wedding.

But first she had to convince Sam that he wanted to marry her. Actually, she wouldn't have to convince him of that part. He already loved her. He'd said so. And because he was thirty, he'd want marriage and kids and a life in that cute little house. She got all warm and fuzzy just thinking about it.

All she really needed to change was Sam's image of her, exactly the way she planned to change his company's image and the image for Slightly Scandalous. But she'd have to do it soon, and she'd have to make an indelible impression, one he wouldn't be able to get out of his mind, ever.

She'd recruit her buddies from work and Sam's brother, Colin. Although she'd met Colin only once, she'd felt an immediate intellectual kinship. She thought Colin would get a real kick out of helping her set a trap for his big brother. And tomorrow night would give her the perfect opportunity.

SAM AGREED to go with Jim and Alicia to the Yucca Lounge, although he'd rather have had a root canal. Every time he looked at Jim, he thought of Kasey, and every time he watched Jim and Alicia getting friendly, he thought of Kasey. On top of that, the whole time he listened to the Tin Tarantulas, he thought of Kasey.

Maybe it didn't matter who he was with or what he was doing. He was doomed to think of Kasey—Kasey on that first night in the hammock, Kasey pushing her sexual limits the second night in her apartment, Kasey prancing down an imaginary runway in crotchless panties, Kasey sobbing as he told her they were finished. He couldn't bring himself to picture Kasey moving on and feeling grateful to him that he'd had the good sense to break up with her. That image hurt too damned much.

One of these days he was bound to feel noble and virtuous for what he'd done. One of these days the pain had to improve—no one could continue to live for very long in this kind of agony. The worst of it was he couldn't tell anyone. The way he saw it, nobody else needed to hear about this, but that meant he couldn't vent, either.

Still, he had the definite feeling that Colin knew
something was wrong. During the break between sets,
he came to the table as usual and tried to act like his
normal wisecracking self. But in unguarded moments
he would look thoughtfully at Sam, and when Sam
caught him at it, he'd turn away and make another
joke. Maybe Kasey had gotten in touch with Colin,
somehow. Maybe she was planning to show up here
tonight.

The more Sam thought about it, the more likely it
seemed that Colin was in on some scheme of Kasey's.
Sam hadn't expected her to give up, although that's
what she should do. If she thought Colin would put in
a good word for her, she might have asked him to do
that after the gig tonight. Well, Colin could talk until he
was blue in the face. Sam was not about to ruin the future of the woman he loved, no matter how much the
decision to let her go hurt.

After the band's final number, Sam braced himself,
convinced that Colin would ambush him, somehow.
Jim and Alicia were ready to leave, but Sam delayed
them, just in case Colin had something to say. It
wouldn't do any good, of course. But if the message
had come from Kasey...aw, hell, who was he kidding?
He wanted to believe that she'd talked to Colin. He
wanted some evidence that she would try to get him
back.

Nothing she could do would work, but still, if she
tried, that would soothe his soul a little bit. He'd hold
her off until she stopped trying and realized that they
didn't belong together. In truth, they *might* have belonged together, if they'd met several years from now.

Maybe he'd look her up after a long time had passed. God knows he wouldn't be with anyone. He couldn't imagine it, not after loving Kasey.

Colin didn't show. Sam finally excused himself from Jim and Alicia and went to find him. There was Colin, surrounded by his female groupies as usual. Sam waded into the middle of them and tapped his brother on the shoulder.

Colin glanced up. "Hey, bro! How come you're still around?"

"I wondered if you wanted to talk to me about anything."

"No, not really." But there was a gleam in his eyes. "Go on home, man. Guys your age need your rest."

Sam's heart leaped. Sure as the world, Colin had loaned Kasey his key to Sam's house, and she was waiting for him. He would bet money on it. "That's what you think," he said, just to test his theory. "Jim, Alicia and I are heading out for a late-night snack." They had no such plan, but he might smoke Colin out that way.

"Suit yourself, dude." Colin tried to look unconcerned.

Sam saw right through him, and excitement fizzed in his veins. Something was definitely going on, and he would find out what once he got home. "See you later," he said to Colin.

"Sure thing. And thanks for coming. The crowd was great."

"Yeah, it was." Sam was happy for his brother. The Yucca Lounge had been packed. But now he had to go home and tell Kasey he really didn't want to see her anymore. He shouldn't be looking forward to that, but the thought of talking to her one more time put a spring in his step as he returned to the table where Jim and Alicia waited.

"We're going out for coffee," Jim said. "Want to come along?"

"Thanks," Sam said, "but if you could drop me at home, I'm ready to turn in." He noticed they took the news with good cheer. No doubt they wanted to be alone, anyway.

When they pulled into his driveway, he looked for Kasey's little red convertible, but it wasn't there. The disappointment was so sharp he almost forgot to say all the usual polite things to Jim and Alicia. At the last minute he remembered to thank them and promised that they'd get together again soon.

Then he started up his walkway. He might actually have to sell the place. That would be stupid, because he hadn't lived in it long enough to build up much equity, but the house no longer interested him if he couldn't have Kasey. Coming home night after night, knowing she'd never be there again, would be pure torture.

After twisting the key in the lock, he opened the door. Monday he'd call a real-estate agent. Monday he'd...

He stood in the doorway, the key still dangling from his hand, while he stared at his living room. Vases and pots of flowers covered every surface. Roses, daisies, chrysanthemums, you name it. They sat on the coffee table, the end tables, even the floor. And sticking out of one bright vase of mixed blooms was a sign. He moved closer. *Let me color your world. Love, Kasey.*

"Kasey?" She must have used the time he was at the Yucca Lounge to set this up. He wasn't sure if she'd staged it and left, or if she was still here. But if she was here, she didn't answer.

Heart pounding, he walked through the living room, picking his way around the flowers. Then he smelled something cooking. Could she be in the kitchen? But she didn't cook. Following the delicious aroma of apple pie, he went through the dining room into the kitchen.

She wasn't there, but the counters were filled with pastries. The aroma he'd caught came from a chafing dish of warm apple cobbler. He leaned over a decorated sheet cake next to it. Was that a naked woman outlined in pink frosting? With little red nipples? It was. Next to it, lettered in red, was the message *Let me cook up some excitement. Love, Kasey.*

So she wasn't in the kitchen, either. He decided to check the bedroom, imagining her stretched out on his king-size mattress. Walking down the hall, he trembled, knowing he needed to be strong, and aware he was weakening fast. But she wasn't in the bedroom, either.

Instead, the bed was mounded with silk pillows. On his dresser and nightstands, dozens of votives in glass holders turned the room into a fairyland. Then he realized each pillow was stitched with a word, and taken together, they spelled out *I can set your nights on fire. Love, Kasey.*

He only had one obvious place left to look. Taking a deep breath, he walked back down the hall and through the kitchen. He opened the door, expecting to find candles there, too. But the area was dark and still.

Sick with disappointment, he stepped onto the patio. He'd been so sure she'd be here, with some sort of grand finale.

Then he heard a click and Bruce Springsteen's "Secret Garden" drifted from somewhere nearby. Next the trees sparkled to life, the branches strung with hundreds of tiny white lights.

"Welcome home, Sam."

He spun around, and she emerged from the shadows wearing the skimpiest halter top and the tightest capri pants he'd ever seen.

He stared at her, at a loss for words.

But she seemed to know exactly what she wanted to say, as if she'd rehearsed it. "Sam, I can be everything you need—a partner, a playmate and a lover. You told me that this sort of happiness doesn't come along every day, and you're right. Are you willing to let me go and take a chance on losing what you've found?"

"But...you're so...young." She didn't seem young right now, though. She seemed exactly the right age for everything he had in mind.

She looked at him, her posture straight, her gaze steady. "I'm old enough to know that I've found the love of my life. Are you old enough to know that?"

He stepped closer, drawn to her by the certainty in her eyes. "I don't want you to regret loving me."

"Never in a million years."

With a groan of surrender, he gathered her into his arms. God, she felt so good. "I need you. I need you desperately."

She held him close and looked deep into his eyes.

"We need each other, Sam. You know we're perfect together. We'd be fools to let anything tear us apart."

He trembled to think how close they'd come to having that happen, all because he'd allowed a numerical age to cloud what he knew about her in his heart. She was his equal in every way, more than his equal in some ways. "I was almost that dumb."

"That's why I had to save you...save us."

A smile of pure joy tugged at his mouth. "You did one helluva job, PR lady."

Her serious expression lifted and her eyes began to sparkle with professional pride. "You liked the way I displayed my message points?"

He tightened his hold on her. "I like the way you display all your points."

"You were one tough customer to deal with, but I have to say, this campaign kicked butt."

"I can't believe you did all this while I was at Colin's gig." And he wondered how easily this outfit of hers came off.

"I had help. I called in my buddies at the office. They gave me a ride here so you wouldn't see my car out front, and then they fetched, carried and decorated. They left about thirty minutes ago."

"So they know about us?" The happiness just kept coming.

"Yes, and it's only the beginning. I have Alicia working on Jim right now, and tomorrow we'll go over and see my parents. You'll need to get reacquainted, and we should take a trip to Oregon."

He started feeling giddy. "We should?"

"Of course. They should meet me before the wedding, don't you think?"

"You're going to marry me?" He forgot all about trying to get her clothes off as he contemplated this new miracle.

"What did you think that little speech of mine was all about?"

"Being perfect for each other. But I thought, since you're so young, that you might want to—" He noticed she was glaring at him. "What?"

She blew out a breath. "First of all, if I never have to hear that phrase *you're so young* again, that would be just ducky. And my speech, you might recall, was about getting *married*, Sam. My message points were about getting married. This whole production is supposed to lead to the conclusion that we'll get married."

"Oh." Life was so good, he could hardly stand it.

"So are you going to propose to me, or not?"

He grinned and cupped her face in both hands. "Not while your face is all scrunched up like that. You might turn me down."

"I will not! I—"

He kissed her, and because she'd had her mouth open, he got immediate entrance, so he could use his tongue to best advantage. By the time he finished with her and lifted his head, her expression was exactly the way he wanted it, dazed and happy. "There," he said. "You hot woman, you. Will you marry me?"

She sighed and pulled his head back down. "Yes, yes, a thousand times yes. I love you so much, Sam."

"And I love you, Kasey," he whispered as his mouth grazed hers. Then he couldn't resist, because after all, she'd practically dared him. "Even if you are so young." Then he gasped as she grabbed his crotch.

"What did you say?" she murmured, laughter in her voice.

"That you're...old enough. Yeah, that's it. Old enough."

"And how about you? Are you old enough to know better?"

"Me, I'm old enough to know the best, and you're it."

"Good answer."

As her grip turned into a caress, he leaned down and whispered a suggestion in her ear. Before long, they were in the bedroom tossing aside silk message pillows so they could set the night on fire exactly as she'd promised. Right before Sam thrust deep inside her, he remembered his words, the ones she'd tossed back at him. *This sort of happiness doesn't come along every day.*

He had a feeling that from now on, it just might.

* * * * *

*Look for Vicki Lewis Thompson's
next bestseller,
The Nerd Who Loved Me,
coming in August 2004 from
St. Martin's Paperbacks*

HARLEQUIN®

Temptation®

When the spirits are willing...
Anything can happen!

Welcome to the Inn at Maiden Falls, Colorado. Once a brothel in the 1800s, the inn is now a successful honeymoon resort. Only, little does anybody guess that all that marital bliss comes with a little supernatural persuasion....

Don't miss this fantastic new miniseries. Watch for:

#977 SWEET TALKIN' GUY by Colleen Collins
June 2004

#981 CAN'T BUY ME LOVE by Heather MacAllister
July 2004

#985 IT'S IN HIS KISS by Julie Kistler
August 2004

THE SPIRITS
ARE WILLING

Available wherever Harlequin books are sold.

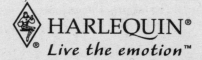

HARLEQUIN®
Live the emotion™

www.eHarlequin.com

HTTSAW

HARLEQUIN®

Temptation®

is turning twenty!

We're young, we're legal (well almost) and we're old enough to get into trouble!

And to celebrate our coming-of-age, we're reintroducing one of our most popular miniseries.

Whenever you want a sassy, sexy book with a little something out of the ordinary, look for...

Don't miss July's pick...

I SHOCKED THE SHERIFF
by MARA FOX

When Roxy Adams shows up in her bright yellow Porsche, Sheriff Luke Hermann knows he and his small Texas town will never be the same. Within twenty-four hours, he's pulled her out of a catfight, almost hauled her off to jail and spent the most incredible moments of his life in her bed. But Luke knows she'll love him and leave him soon enough. Still, before she does, he intends to make sure she'll miss being held in the long arms of the law....

Available wherever Harlequin books are sold.

www.eHarlequin.com

HTECSTS

HARLEQUIN®

Temptation.

COMING NEXT MONTH

#981 CAN'T BUY ME LOVE Heather MacAllister
The Spirits Are Willing

Lawyer Alexis O'Hara is tired of the dating, mating, then hating game. She wants to settle down, and this time she's not getting her heart involved. Her mentor Vincent Cathardy seems like a perfect husband and the Inn at Maiden Falls seems like a perfect place. Only, she hasn't counted on running into an old flame…or getting some supernatural "persuasion" to rekindle the fires of first love….

#982 I SHOCKED THE SHERIFF Mara Fox
Editor's Choice

When Roxy Adams shows up in her bright yellow Porsche, Sheriff Luke Hermann knows he and his small Texas town will never be the same. Within twenty-four hours he's pulled her out of a catfight, almost hauled her off to jail and spent the most incredible moments of his life in her bed. But Luke knows she'll love him and leave him soon enough. Still, before he does, he intends to make sure she'll miss being held in the long arms of the law….

#983 HER FINAL FLING Joanne Rock
Single in South Beach

Christine Chandler is here to do a job that could make her fledgling landscaping company a success. And that job doesn't include entertaining advances from a globe-trotting hottie just filling in his time. Doesn't matter how sexy—or how tempting—Vito Cesare is, she's not about to take him up on his offers. But before she knows what's happening, he's made her one seductive offer she can't refuse!

#984 EVERY STEP YOU TAKE… Liz Jarrett

Paige Harris has found sanctuary at the Sunset Café in Key West, Florida. Waitressing tables, she's hiding out from her powerful ex-fiancé. Luckily, undercover P.I. Max Walker's on the case. Paige can't help but notice his handsome face and the hot body that goes with it. Though he's her secret protector, there's nothing secret about the scorching heat between them….